HARD TO TAKE

DENVER KODIAKS

BOOK TWO

PIPER LAWSON

Content editing by Becca Mysoor
Line and copy editing by Cassie Robertson
Proofreading by Devon Burke
Cover design by Emily Wittig

HARD TO TAKE

DENVER KODIAKS #2

My fake boyfriend is now...my new roommate?

Miles Garrett, pro basketball player and star of every one of my fantasies, has decided I'm moving in with him.

My brother's teammate has always protected me out of loyalty. He makes me feel like everything will be okay even when my life is on fire.

But when he looks at me, I wonder what it would be like if he was truly mine. If I had the dream life and dream job and the dream guy.

Did I mention we can't keep our hands off each other?

I hoped the proximity would get him out of my system. Turns out sharing a bedroom wall changes hungry looks and brushes in the hall into sweaty sessions and late-night confessions.

Miles keeps my secrets and sees me like no one else.

Too bad the playoffs are coming up and my brother doesn't know.

The truth is going to be hard to take.

Hard to Take is a pro basketball romance with banter, spice, and all the swoony vibes! It's the second book in the Denver Kodiaks series. Miles and Brooke's addictive story begins in Hard to Fake and concludes in Hard to Break.

TROPES:

- brother's best friend
- roommates
- pro athlete hero
- cinnamon roll hero
- he's always wanted her
- sassy heroine
- college crush
- secret dating

For every woman who wants
a sexy pro athlete roommate to make her elite lattes.

BROOKE

S weat. Heat. Longing.

Miles's hands span my waist. His rough palm across my stomach heats my skin, sparking a thrum of desire that streaks lower as he bends his head between my thighs.

Then all I feel is his tongue.

This man's fucking tongue teases me, sending jolts of electricity that make me arch against him as my hands fist in the sheets.

"How do I know it's not fake?"

The woman's voice over the phone snaps me out of my fantasy. I narrowly avoid tripping on a crack in the curb, my suede knee-high Stuart Weitzman boots saving me from tossing the two coffees stacked and balanced in a gloved hand.

"It's genuine." I catch my breath from the near miss. "Last season's hottest seller. You carry this bag and everyone will notice."

The woman buying my designer purse considers. "Do you have more pictures of the interior?"

I glance up at a street sign. I'm half a dozen blocks from my destination, so I pull up at a corner and click into my photos.

Vail, the Kappa retreat and my failed attempt to land a brand deal with my sorority sister's company feel a hundred years rather than one week in the past.

But rent is due and I had to take the gut-wrenching step of starting to sell off my wardrobe.

"Here you go." I hit Send on an image of the inside of the bag.

My gaze is pulled to the top of my cracked phone screen and one of the pictures Miles and I took on that rooftop when we were pretending to be dating.

He's behind me, his arms around me, his cheek pressed to mine. It's not even our closeness but the expression on his face that hits me. His wide grin and the way he holds me tight say I'm everything he wants and he's never letting me go.

The cold air sticks in my throat.

"Would you take five hundred? It's not really my color but I could dye it."

Her request is devastating. At least we're not on a video call so she can't see me cringe. "Seven hundred. And if you're set on dying it, for the love of Gucci, don't do it yourself. I'll give you the name of a guy who does customizations."

We make plans for her to pick it up and I click off moments before I brush through the doors of my friend's studio, coffees balanced in one hand.

"Hi, beautiful!" Nova rises to greet me. "I'm covered in paint," she warns.

"Paint is temporary. Friendship is forever." I hug her before nodding toward her work-in-progress, an abstract swirl of colors. "What's this?"

"Trying something new." She accepts the coffee with a grateful hum.

My friend's career is still on the rise, but she's best known for more literal images, including the massive installation at the Kodiaks' arena featuring the starters from last year's winning team. This is softer and more organic.

"I like it. It's a whole new Nova."

She laughs. "Thanks. But let's not pretend that my latest painting is the most important thing we need to discuss." Her eyes brighten. "I haven't seen you all week and you owe me major details. What happened at the retreat?!"

My heart kicks against my ribs as memories rise up without permission.

The way he charmed every Kappa and her date and defended me against my enemies.

The feel of his mouth on mine in the coat closet.

The way he touched me in the bed we were never supposed to share.

"Miles was the perfect boyfriend, in public and private. Right up until he left in the middle of the night."

Her eyes widen. "He didn't say anything?"

"A one-sentence note on hotel stationary about sending me a limo and seeing me when I got back to Denver."

Nova taps her chin. "But you haven't talked since?"

I shake my head.

When I got back to Denver in the limo Miles sent, it wasn't my fake boyfriend but my brother who opened the door.

"We need to talk." Jay's face was determined and a little angry.

"About?" I shifted out, shoving down the

emotions ricocheting around my body as he helped me get my bag out of the trunk.

"Mom. She's asking me to do all this stuff for her campaign. Like she doesn't understand that I have a job."

Relief edged in.

Not about Miles.

"How did you handle her when she was like this?" he went on, oblivious.

"I did what she wanted." I headed for the door of my building. Jay trailed me, carrying my suitcase.

In the elevator, and I swiveled to face my brother. "My turn. Did Miles hit Kevin back in college?"

As the doors slid closed, Jay realized he was trapped. Even though he had a few inches on me, I had him pinned with my eyes.

"I was worried about you when I got drafted," Jay said at last. "I asked him to check on you. I didn't trust Kevin with you, even before the coke."

The elevator reached my floor and dinged.

I lunged into the hall after my brother. "And that warranted Miles beating the crap out of him?"

Jay stopped and turned to face me. "Miles found out about what Kevin did. He wanted to make sure Kevin stayed away. Think he took it a little far."

My brother's admission had my insides twisting.

That was why Miles had shown up back in college, why he had taken me for breakfast, why he had acted as though he cared.

"So you told him to watch my back three years ago."

Jay frowned. "Might have mentioned it a time or two since."

My heart plummeted.

That was what the entire weekend with Miles at the retreat had been about.

Loyalty between teammates. One friend having another's back.

It had never been about me.

"The team's been on the road all week, but they come home tonight." Nova's voice brings me back.

The thought has crossed my mind. Miles will be in the same city, and we'll be back in the same circles. He's almost painfully accessible.

"There's no reason for me to talk to him," I tell Nova as I pick at the edges of my manicure. "My brother asked Miles to keep an eye on me. I was a favor for a teammate. Anything that happened between us was fake. Exactly like it was supposed to be."

Nova doesn't look convinced.

My phone buzzes.

Speak of the devil.

"Is that him?" Nova prompts.

"Yes." Part of me wants to hear his voice, but there's nothing I need from him. I tuck the phone in in my pocket, letting it go to voicemail.

"I'm over it. He did what I needed him to do. We can go back to—"

"Looking too long at one another across every room you're both in? Flirting incessantly? Single-handedly making me want to write fanfic?"

I glare at my friend. "Nothing. We can go back to being nothing."

I'm not taking any more calls from my brother's guard dog. Not losing any more sleep on a crush that has lasted longer than my favorite pair of shoes.

At least I've made enough to cover my rent for the month.

Nova and I finish our coffee talking about more pleasant topics and I head home.

On my way, I send a text to my landlord to tell him I'll have my December rent payment to him tomorrow.

A message comes back.

Rent is going up January 1.

"You've got to be fucking kidding me."

MILES

Hoopsnews Update: Kodiaks Cling To Third In The West Heading Into Holidays

"Three wins in a row, baby! That's what you call a streak," Rookie hollers.

"Sit your short-attention-span ass on the bench and I'll show you a streak," Damon, one of our new guys, counters.

The Kodiaks are clustered around our gym, warmed up and ready to practice.

The last week of wins should have me riding high, especially since we got them on other teams' home courts.

Somehow, the grin that usually comes as easily as breathing still takes effort.

"The road trip had some positive signs." Coach addresses us from the front of practice. "But we need reinforcements." He turns to the head trainer intently, willing him for good news.

Heading into December, the first six weeks of the season are finished and we're starting to see what kind of team we have.

And, almost as important, what kind of team everyone else has.

We're midway up the standings, which is midway down depending on how you look at it. It's good enough to still be in line for a playoff spot, but it's not enough to stop the talk that we won't repeat as champions.

"It's going to be a few more weeks before Atlas is back in workouts," our trainer informs us.

Jay covers his face with both hands as he paces. Clay shifts back in his chair, jaw working.

Rookie throws a towel at Atlas, who lifts both hands as if to say, "Not my fault."

Our bench guys mutter to one another. Winning pro basketball games is hard as hell.

"We've got Boston to look forward to soon, and I

don't have to tell you how tough they are. Especially this year." Coach folds his arms.

"I can take Hawkins," Jay tosses.

"Not what he's saying," Rookie says under his breath.

Jay growls.

Marcus Hawkins is Boston's new point guard, traded from Philly. He took a strong team and made them even more dangerous.

More than that, the guy likes to talk trash.

I figured after the first couple weeks of the season, the media narratives about us being a one hit wonder would have faded.

Instead, they've been sharpened by the addition of an unofficial figurehead: Hawkins.

He shoots his mouth off at every opportunity.

Coaching staff is too new.

Clay Wade is on his way out.

Ellis and Garrett can't cut it against all-star guards.

He's a one-man hot take machine. They're the kind of sound bites that would make my teeth grind together if I was a less chill guy.

No matter what's going on outside, the basketball court is where I'm at home. There's nothing as soothing as the sound of sneakers on floors, the smell of wax and sweat, the feel of the perfect three rolling off your fingertips.

For the next hour and a half, we're focused.

"Ellis and Garrett." Jay's head and mine snap toward Coach at the end. "You were a step slow connecting. Let's fix it before it becomes more of a problem."

We're back in the locker room, when Jay says, "We should go out tonight."

"We shouldn't," Clay murmurs.

"We've earned it. It's good for morale," Jay argues. He turns to me, waiting for my backup.

"I'm beat. Going to run some things over to Grams, then crash." I grab a towel and head for the shower.

Since the hospital called me in the middle of the night in Vail, I've been dealing with Grams.

It hasn't been the easiest thing given we've been on the road most of the week, but I've called the hospital and the retirement home often enough that they probably curse the second they see me on the call display.

"Broken wrist," the doctors said.

Given the fall, it could've been worse.

Yet since she's been in a cast, she seems to have gotten more active and opinionated. From the second

I drove her home, she's been determined to prove to the entire world she's stronger than ever.

I need to get her into a better situation with more care.

I even thought about moving her into my place, but I can't care for her the way she needs and don't have time to try to find or interview potential staff to help her when I'm not there.

Still, there's another situation that's got me tossing and turning.

Brooke Ellis.

My teammate's little sister.

The woman I can't get out of my head.

I slept with Brooke in Vail.

Wish I could chalk it up to getting her out of my system, but even before she kissed me in that hot tub and I practically dragged her back to our room, I was way too invested.

Thing is, she hasn't seemed interested in talking since.

I tried calling her this week.

Not once, but three times.

Maybe her phone's broken.

When I get out of the shower, my phone's lit up with texts from the BearFam chat.

Jay: We should go out tonight. Who's in?

Chloe: Ownership has a new advertiser I'm trying to recruit.

Rookie: It'll keep til tomorrow. B?

Brooke: I'm auditioning roommates.

I'm about to drop my phone in my bag when the message comes through.

So much for her phone being broken.

"Since when is little sis looking for a roommate?" I ask Jay, who's getting dressed at his locker a couple down from mine.

My voice is completely level.

No, fuck level, I sound *amused*, as though it's cute she's thinking of sleeping next to a complete stranger, of sharing her space—her life—with someone she hardly knows.

Jay lifts a shoulder and types.

Jay: Since when are you getting a roommate?

Brooke: Since I realized I miss having Nova as my roommate and need some company in my 2 BR.

Rookie: You accepting applications? I don't need to sleep in the second BR. We can share :D

Jay: Only sleep you'll be doing is in a coma.

She doesn't want to come to me?

No sweat.

I've never had to chase down a woman before.

But then, Brooke makes me do a lot of things I've never done.

Mile High is our place, but once in a while, we like to go somewhere with dance music.

Being in a club makes me feel twenty-two again. No matter how much a drink costs, I can't get over the floors, the flashing lights, or the pulsing EDM that makes my eardrums vibrate like the Kodiak Arena shaking during finals last year.

Can't remember the last time we were here. It was definitely before we started our new season, and Atlas got hurt, and Brooke asked me to pretend to be her fake boyfriend, and I got the call in the middle of the night about my grams.

It feels like forever ago.

"If I were an animal, I'd be a goat," Rookie calls over the music.

"You're saying that because want to be *the* G.O.A.T., which you've got to earn," Damon shouts back.

"You planning to steal that title while Clay's asleep? Because if he's awake, you're going to have to fight him for it," Jay points out.

"Anytime, anywhere. But as a backup, I'd be an ostrich. Fast as fuck and scary too." The guys laugh and Rookie turns to me. "What about you?"

There are plenty of fans here to stroke my ego. Before I can respond, one of them grabs my arm, smiling up at me.

"You're Miles Garrett! I started watching basketball because of you," a brunette calls over the music.

"Oh yeah? Tell me what you learned."

I'm a personable guy, and being nice to fans is a knee-jerk reaction.

"Basketball players are really big. Pretty much all over six feet." She announces it as if she's discovered a new wonder of the world. "They're probably big everywhere."

My gaze is scanning the club, but the innuendo hits me over the head.

"Stands to reason."

None of this interaction takes a single ounce of my attention when Brooke walks in the door with Sierra and Nova.

Her hair is down in wild curls around her head. Her lips are dark against her golden skin, her eyes lined. Her black dress is sparkly, dipping low between her perfect breasts and ending high on her toned thighs.

Thank fuck for whatever designer made heels that tall. Makes it easier for a big guy like me to see and appreciate every inch of her.

It's been a week since I've seen her. The social posts I shamelessly watched for clues to her state of mind and simply to look at her don't count.

She's alive and grinning and gorgeous.

Suddenly, I'm picturing her on her knees, her fingers wrapped around me. The heat of her mouth, the sounds she'd make as if she knew exactly what she was doing, taking me apart one wet stroke at a—

Shit. This went south fast.

Her eyes find me and there's not enough air in my lungs.

She could do any number of things. Roll her eyes, shake her pretty head. Slice through the crowd on her high heels and press up to yell in my ear what an asshole I am.

I want her to.

Instead, she turns away.

In the dark I can admit I'm a little sore about it.

Yeah, I bailed early on our weekend, but I had my reasons. She hasn't given me time to explain. I thought she knew me better than that.

I'm tempted to drag her into a hallway where she can only hear me, that's impossible with the entire team around us.

A rough purring noise interrupts my thoughts. After a beat, I realize it's coming from the woman I converted to basketball.

"Are you okay?" I ask, concerned. Maybe she's having some kind of allergic reaction.

"I'm growling. Like a bear's mating call." She blinks thick eyelashes at me.

My gaze drags back to Brooke, who's moving toward the bar.

"Bears usually vocalize when they're feeling

18

threatened," I offer before cutting through the crowd toward Brooke.

From behind, I get a chance to look at her as she pushes her hair over one shoulder. Her skin is damp with sweat.

"You dodging my calls?" I'm trying to sound as though I don't care if the answer is yes or no.

She glances back. "Been busy."

Any other girl, I'd take it at face value, but she responds to people she cares about. She responds when something matters.

The bartender sets four glasses in front of her—for her, Nova, Sierra, and Chloe, I'm guessing. Brooke tries to grab them all at once. The final glass wobbles precariously.

I step in, taking it before she can stop me. "Figured you might want to thank me for coming to that reunion with you. Braving an entire resort full of strangers to save your ass."

"Except they weren't strangers, were they? You were already acquainted with everyone from Kappa. Especially Kevin."

His name on her lips throws what I was about to say out the window. My gut clenches. "Whatever he said, Princess—"

"He didn't say anything. Caroline told me you

hit him."

Damn it.

That's worse, because it means the piece of shit talked to someone.

He wasn't supposed to let that get around. It was the only thing we agreed on, for mutually beneficial reasons.

"Brooke," I start.

"Did he hit you first?"

My head falls back.

"It doesn't matter," she shouts. "Jay explained why you did it. You don't owe me anything."

She pushes past me, starting for her friends who're leaning against the railing around the dance floor.

The pulsing beat throbs through my feet. I feel it more and more the closer we get to the floor.

A crowd passes in front of her, forcing us to bunch up. My fingers wrap around her arm and tug her back until she hits my chest.

"What's with this roommate business?" I call next to her ear as we wait for the path to clear. "Don't tell me it was brought on by some sudden 'I miss sharing a bathroom with another human' bullshit."

The comment earns me side-eye. "My rent's

going up, and I didn't get the deal with Elise. She picked Caroline over me."

Surprise sets me back. "Because?"

"Caroline had this video from the retreat." Brooke turns back toward the crowd.

She's trying to look unaffected, but in profile, I see the hurt underneath.

There's only one thing Caroline could've had video of.

Our time in the hot tub comes back to me, the heat of it, the longing. The absolute fuck-everyone-else of it, because it was Brooke and me and it was enough.

This is my fault.

I wanted to help her, and instead, I let my damned hunger for her block out everything else.

"I'll pay your rent," I call over the music.

"Yeah, no." She laughs in my face. "You're not my boyfriend, real or fake. The gig is over."

She shifts the two drinks into one arm and grabs the other from me, then pushes through the crowd to her friends.

What is it with this girl?

Never figured I had a thing for stubborn, independent women. With Brooke, I can't decide if it's a feature or a bug.

Two more beers disappear in a heartbeat.

"It's nothing, right?" I look up to see Jay at my shoulder.

"What?"

"What Coach said. That you and me are a step slow."

"Of course not. It was a couple of missed connections. My head's been all over with my grams."

He nods slowly.

"This is about Hawkins shooting his mouth off," I guess.

Jay smooths a hand over his braids. "Nah. Just a long road to playoffs. A lot on my shoulders."

"Not only yours," I remind him. "We'll get there."

I'm a little drunk and can't resist saying, "You're going to talk her out of this shit, right?"

He follows my gaze toward where Brooke is dancing, her hands in the air and her smile flashing bright in the lights.

"She wants to live with a rando. That's how bad things happen." Triggering her brother's fears isn't the most aboveboard way to crack down on this, but it'll have to do.

He squares to face me. "She asked me to be more trusting, and she told me to back off."

"Then move her in with you," I try.

"My place is getting renovated. She doesn't want the construction in her face."

So much for Jay helping.

"Hey," I go on, the beer definitely going to my head. "What did you tell her about what happened with Kevin? You know, so we're all on the same page."

He blinks at me. "The truth."

Right.

Because we all have the same version of what went down.

As I nurse another beer and watch her without looking like I am, I know she's going to ignore my advice from earlier like she ignores every other thing she doesn't want to hear.

It's obvious she wants nothing to do with me, and getting inside her stubborn head is harder than breaking into the NBA.

Yeah, well, two can be stubborn.

There's one option. It's an obvious overstepping of any boundaries between us.

Princess is going to hate it.

I'm fine with that.

BROOKE

"So, why are you *really* getting a roommate?"

Nova holds the door for me as we step inside the donut shop. The place is decorated in pink and white and has a long line. The glass cases lining the front are packed full of beautiful pastries.

"I meant what I said in the group chat. I miss having someone in my space. I should have thought of it sooner."

"It's not because your mom cut you off?" Nova always says what she's thinking.

Missing out on the deal with Elise threw me, but it exposed the bigger problem beyond making enough influencer money to pay my rent month to month: I want a career that makes me unshakeable so that even when life sends me on a rollercoaster, I don't have to run to my mom or brother.

Losing to Caroline didn't send me spinning out—it lit a fire under my ass. I need to figure out my way forward.

But it's a lot easier to do that with a roof over my head, and splitting the bill is the only practical way to do that if I'm not willing to go into debt.

We reach the front of the line and order a fluffy donut for each of us. Mine has white icing and raspberries, and hers has caramel drizzle and brownies.

We take our treats to an available table.

"I put an ad online and have a bunch of interested people, even after weeding out the weirdest ones. The first person is coming over tonight."

I slide into my seat, brushing my ponytail behind me.

"Are you sure about this?" She shifts forward, her big eyes widening. "Because our new house—"

"I'm not moving in with you and your husband! I love you for offering, but that's final."

Nova sighs so I continue.

"I said I wanted a roommate, and Clayton Wade does not fit the bill. He's too broody. He'd bring down the entire vibe." I tilt my head. "Besides, you guys are in the honeymoon bliss phase. Enjoy it."

"It has been pretty great," she admits. "I thought things would calm down after we got married, especially with the season. I miss him when he's gone, but when he gets home..." Her eyes drift closed.

"Not envious at all that you're having an orgasm just thinking about it." I take a bite of the donut and the sticky sweetness melts in my mouth. "Mmmm. Speaking of, this is amazing."

She mumbles her agreement as I look around. Usually, I'm the one who's up to date on the new places.

"I'm so proud you discovered this."

"I've been doing more on social media. Which has upsides and downsides."

Now I'm curious. My friend sounds stressed, but building a brand and managing an image feel more like a game to me.

She pulls up her phone. "I started doing these AMAs, and mostly I get great things, but once in a while someone will say something shitty."

"What kind of shitty?"

I look at her screen at the messages.

You haven't made anything new in forever. Are you retired?

How can you call yourself a real artist?

I can't believe you took Clayton Wade off the market.

I hate that trolls are dragging her down. I might not have superpowers, but I can fix this.

"For the first question, you can address it with a picture of you working." I grab one from her file and post it, along with the caption "WIP. Top secret."

"But I haven't made anything new this week."

"Doesn't matter. You're working on your own schedule and cycle, and that's good enough."

The relief on her expression is evident.

"These other questions don't need to be dealt with. More than that, you don't need to look at these. You should have someone to deal with them for you. If it was me, I'd post a picture of you and Clay with a peace emoji and say the man is yours, and he's the lucky one and it's the last you're speaking on it."

She laughs. "I like that. You're really good at this. Have you thought about doing PR?"

"Trust me, I'm busy enough trying to keep my own account from turning into a dumpster fire."

Still, it was more fun to help her than figure out next steps with my own brand.

"At the risk of overstepping, I asked Clay about Miles," she says.

"Tell me you did not ask your husband for inside information on his teammate." I take an increased interest in the sprinkles dotting my donut, picking off a single colorful stick and popping it in my mouth.

"I absolutely did and I'd do it again. Especially the way Miles was looking at you at the club." Nova's smile fades a little. "Clay said Miles has been skipping out on team stuff to visit his grandmother. Apparently she just got out of the hospital."

My stomach plummets.

He tried to talk to me, on the phone and at the club, but I was too busy being cool and unaffected by his hotness and oblivious to the Kodashians drooling on his shoes to ask him.

I check the time on my phone. "I need to go meet this potential roommate. Wish me luck."

But as I head for the door, I type out a text three times before I hit Send.

Brooke: Nova told me about your Grams. Is she okay?

Inviting a stranger to become my roommate might not have been my plan at the start of the year, but I'm starting to see the value of it. First and foremost, it will give me a break on my "How the hell did I not realize it was that much?!" rent while I figure out my new career.

When the knock comes on my door, I'm not ready, but I told the concierge I was expecting company and to send them up.

The apartment looks great. I added a couple of new plants whose names I've forgotten to make the place more vibrant. I'm still wearing leggings and a tank top from meeting Nova, but I put on makeup and pulled my favorite slouchy camel sweater over my head.

I figured it would feel more welcoming if I moved my stuff out of the closet in the second room—it's Realtor 101. I want my new roomie to picture themselves in the space, so I put my stuff in boxes but haven't had time to move them to my room.

My sweater slips off one shoulder as I cross to the foyer. I square my shoulders, ready to be welcoming and approachable.

Showtime.

I pull the door wide and fix on a smile.

"Hey! I'm Brooke..." I open the door and my smile fades with shock.

It's not the engineering grad student I expected.

Instead, the Kodiaks' shooting guard stares down at me from that layer of stratosphere he occupies seemingly without any effort.

Miles's hair is a mess, his blue eyes electric. He takes up the entire hallway. In sweatpants and a hoodie, he could've come from the gym, except he's clearly had a shower.

He flashes a smile.

"Hey. I'm Miles."

Three words. They affect me more than they should.

It's his voice, the smoothness of it. It feels as if he's stroking my skin.

Heat curls low in my stomach even before I can shove the thought down.

I resist the temptation to play with the cuffs of my sweater. I'm not a self-conscious teen. I'm a composed twenty-something woman in her own home.

And the last time we were alone, both of us were naked.

Waffles barks up at me from Miles's side. I crouch and scratch him behind the ears. His soft fur calms my emotions as he leans into my hand with a little grunt.

"Smart," I say.

"What's that?"

"Bringing the dog." Waffles snuffles up at me as if he knows we're talking about him. "What are you doing here?"

Miles is already walking past me into the apartment. "You texted me."

"Oh, honey. That's the beauty of texts. You don't need to respond face to face. You can do it right in the app."

"Same with phone calls, Princess." He beams, giving Midwestern-fucking-farmboy as he reminds me of the three voicemails I didn't return.

It should be annoying. It's oddly endearing.

I glance down the hall. No sign of my future roommate, so for now I let the door swing shut.

"I have a potential roommate coming any minute."

"That's what we need to talk about." His eyes darken, and for a moment, I have the crazy feeling I'm not the only one who's been replaying our night together.

"You're not getting a roommate," he says. "There are all kinds of crazy people that could show up at your door."

"I see that. And you're here to explain that to me in your capacity as...?" I look him up and down.

A beat passes. Two. "A friend."

I remember his fingers digging into my legs. Those smoky blue eyes staring up at me from between my thighs, daring me not to melt under him.

"Well, the roommate thing is not up for negotiation, but I could use a hand."

I bend down to gather Waffles up into my arms, the dog sighing happily as I turn and head farther into my apartment.

Miles trails me into the second bedroom and grabs a box.

"Nova told me about your grandmother," I say, stroking the Frenchie behind the ears. "Is she all right?"

He shifts the heavy box without flinching. "She fell again. They called me Saturday night in Vail after you were already asleep and I didn't want to wake you. When they said she was in the hospital, it was like I went numb. I came straight back."

I stare at him for a minute before realizing he's still holding the massive load.

The box must weigh fifty pounds, but he's not winded at all.

"Um... Put it in the closet. Please," I add, nodding to my room because my own hands are full.

Of course, he came back given that.

It doesn't change the fact that Miles's loyalty is to my brother, but it's hard to fault him for loyalty when he's so devoted, just like with his grandmother. The way he goes to the wall for people he loves.

"How is she?" I ask.

"Improving. Though she's not the world's best patient." His slow smile is wry.

"Does she have scans? I can ask Ruby if she'd take a look for a second opinion." Working in the ER, she sees broken bones all the time.

His eyes crinkle at the corners. "Thanks."

Waffles starts to squirm in my arms, possibly responding to the hammering of my heart as I stare at his owner. I set him down.

"Listen," Miles says after a minute. "In the spirit of friendship, you waking up alone is not what I pictured for the morning after."

His usually casual voice has an edge, as if he's still not convinced of his words even after they're out.

I arch a brow. "We hooked up, Garrett. It was the environment and the hot air balloon thing and the high of pulling one over on Caroline and Kevin. It's not a big deal."

"It's not," he echoes, gaze intensifying.

"No," I say firmly. I'm giving us both an out. "There's another box."

33

He doesn't complain, just heads for the spare room and returns a moment later.

He drops the box in the middle of my room with a thud and surveys my room: the pale pink walls, my bed with its white Pottery Barn duvet, my desk, my art prints. He crosses to the Kodiaks photo on my dresser. It was taken after finals, with the team and all the friends and family. "You have a picture of me in your room."

"It's a picture of my brother," I correct. "And me."

He lifts it anyway, his mouth curving. "I like it."

His thumb moves over the glass. Miles is happy everyone's together and smiling. It's painfully obvious how much that means to him.

"I'll help you interview roommates," he says. "I have a good sense about people."

The change of directions sets me back.

He's actually being sweet. It's harder to argue with him when he's sweet.

"You don't need to do that. I'm not your problem," I remind him, my voice softer now.

He sets down the photo and faces me. "Maybe I want you to be."

My feet are stuck to the floor as if I've stepped in gum.

Except I'm wearing socks, which means it's his words, his expression, that make it impossible for my limbs to move.

He doesn't mean it the way it sounds, but damn, it's hard to remember that when warmth creeps up my body, starting at my toes. It has my fingers tingling, my lips parting.

Before I can respond, there's a new knock on the door.

I grab Miles's arm. "That's Hunter! Lay low. Hide. Something until he's gone."

"Hunter?! You invited a dude to see your place. A stranger." The sweetness is gone, replaced by incredulity. I've never seen his brows so close to his hairline.

I lift my hands. "I'm very inclusive."

Miles grabs my wrist and jerks me back so that I collide with his chest. It's so sudden I don't have time to prepare for the feel of him, the masculine scent, the closeness of his mouth, and the feel of his fingers on my pulse.

"You're not doing this, Princess." His voice is firm.

My lips tip up, intentionally casual despite the hammering of my heart. "Garrett?"

His grip on me tightens. "Yeah."

"Watch me."

I use surprise to my advantage and slip his grip. I run to the door and open it to find a startlingly attractive guy.

"Hey," Hunter says, grinning a blindingly white smile.

"Hey, Hunter! I'm Brooke. So nice to meet you in person. Let me give you a tour."

I start to show him the kitchen. It's going fine until the hairs on my neck lift. I feel Miles at my back before I hear him.

"She snores," comes his voice from behind me.

My eyes shut briefly as Hunter laughs. When I blink them open, he's casting a wary look between us. "I can take it. Are you the boyfriend?"

"No. He's a friend," I say firmly, using Miles's word. "*Was* a friend. Whether he's still a friend will depend very much on the next few minutes," I add under my breath.

I motion past Miles, and Hunter comes with me.

"This would be your room. I'm getting things out of the closet," I say.

"It looks great."

Miles leans an arm pleasantly and a little threateningly against the doorframe.

"How tall are you, man?" Hunter asks.

"Six-four. And a half."

"*And a half*," I mutter to myself.

"Your room's on the other side of this wall?" Hunter says.

"Yeah. I'll try to keep it down."

"No worries. You can keep me up anytime."

"Excuse us, Hunter." Miles grabs my arm and drags me to my room and into the walk-in closet.

It all happens so fast I don't have time to hit the light switch, and when he shuts the door, we're in blackness. He crowds my space, forcing my chin up even though I can't see him.

"He's not moving in with you." His breath is gentle on my face, but his tone is seething.

"Hunter is great," I say cheerfully.

"He wants to fuck you."

The tone sets my teeth on edge.

"Just because a pleasant, attractive guy wants to move in doesn't mean he wants to fuck me."

I start to reach for the light switch by the door and trip over something. Miles grabs me in the dark.

I'm momentarily grateful—until, instead of releasing me, he drags me closer—close enough my breasts brush his hard, ribbed stomach.

"You sure about that?" His voice is irritated and possessive at once.

My traitorous nipples harden at the contact.

I'm tall enough that I don't spend a lot of time looking up at anyone, even basketball players. Usually I'm in heels, but my toes curl against the carpet.

In the dark, I can't see him but God, can I feel him.

His fingers press into my ass. His breathing is shallow in a way I've only heard it in the on-court interviews at the end of the fourth quarter in a tough game.

Every moment of our night together in Vail comes rushing back.

I want to feel it all again.

"Brooke?"

Hunter's voice sounds far away but it snaps me out of the moment.

I wrench myself out of Miles's grip and reach for the door.

"I can't believe you live alone," Hunter says from my doorway when I emerge, as if it's totally normal for a woman to emerge from a shut closet. "It's so big. And nice."

Miles makes a sound like a growl at my back. I toss a glare over my shoulder before turning back to Hunter, who at last looks slightly surprised to see the huge man who tumbled out of the closet with me.

"Hunter, you can start filling out the application." I walk him to the couch, then go back to my room and shut the door. "You don't get to tell me what to do," I inform Miles, who's wearing holes in the carpet.

Especially since his interest in my life and well-being is attached to my brother.

I stare at the floor as Waffles circles my legs. I hoist him in my arms, scratching behind his ears.

"Now that your hands are busy, let me say this," Miles starts. "You're too proud. You want to look out for yourself to a fault. But I'm looking out for you, Brooke. Whether you want me to or not."

"By scaring off prospective roommates?" I accidentally squeeze Waffles hard enough he lets out a little grunt of protest.

"There will be no roommates. No rando is finding his way into your room at night. You're moving in with me."

I blink as if it's my vision and not my hearing I'm second-guessing right now.

Miles Garrett is a player. One of the biggest players around.

The idea of him taking a roommate is ludicrous.

Sure, he's a fundamentally decent guy behind the broad smile and the cut body and the huge...

Everything.

Point is, there are a thousand reasons that spell disaster for my sanity and my life.

"There's no way," I scoff as I set Waffles down, stroking his soft fur because it keeps me from smacking his owner. "I need a certain setup for my work."

I'm reaching. I remember every inch of his place, and it was pristine, spacious, and more than comfortable.

"I have an extra bedroom. My building is in a prime location. And," he pauses for emphasis, "I make an *elite* latte."

Hunter knocks on the door, looking in with a tentative smile. "Am I interrupting?"

"Yes."

"No," I say, and Miles frowns.

"Come to my place tomorrow and look around," he insists.

I straighten, aware of Hunter hovering by the door. "It might not measure up."

There's a spark of mischief in his eyes when Miles glances at the other man, then turns back to me. "You've seen the goods, Princess. Seemed to measure up fine."

4

MILES

"*E*veryone wants Park Place, but real players know the value of a railroad." I bump a set of houses with a finger and send them sprawling across the coffee table.

The Parker Brothers did not have basketball-player-sized hands.

"That means they're all mine," Grams decides.

"Nice try." I reach for the nearest pieces and set them back on the Monopoly board as she glares at her cast.

The doctors suggested a cast instead of surgery for the break and since I've gotten back to Denver, I'm doing everything I can to keep her distracted from her new hindrance.

"It itches! Lord. Never had so much itching except this one time your grandfather and I—"

"With all due respect Grams, we're verging on too much information territory." She smiles. "But for real, you haven't taken any of those pain meds, and there's no shame in it. In fact, an anti-inflammatory would help with—"

"If I want your opinion on my inflammation, I will ask you for it," she says tartly. "How's basketball this week?"

"It's a grind with Atlas still injured, but we're hanging in."

She leans in. "Atlas, like the statue that held up the world on his shoulders?"

"Yeah. I'm trying to step up. Not sure my shoulders are as wide."

"It's more about heart than shoulders," she decides.

My mouth curves. "Not sure that's true when it comes to outright feats of strength, but I appreciate the sentiment."

Spectators think playing pro ball is like a TV movie where a bunch of underdogs can come together with heart and a little luck to beat out the competition.

We did have some magic last year in our first championship run.

Thing is, it's only an upset when no one sees you coming.

This season when we roll into a city, they've got a fifty-page scouting report on every Kodiak on the roster.

The opposing teams know all my stats. Hell, they probably know what I eat for breakfast and where I get my hair cut.

"How's Brooke?" Grams asks.

"Fantastic."

She laughs. "That's what you said when I used to ask how your homework was in middle school, which means she's a problem you haven't started solving yet."

Brooke's not a problem—she's my main preoccupation every second I'm not playing ball or with my grams.

"She's moving in with me."

Grams's eyes light up brighter than I've seen them since before I got back to find her in the hospital, pale and disoriented in a gown and with some gnarly-looking X-rays.

"She needs someone," I hear myself say. "She gets into trouble, and I like watching her do it, but..."

I spot a lone hotel under the edge of the sofa and bend to grab it. "Only if I'm there to pick up the pieces."

I tried to be the good guy, helping Brooke interview prospective roommates. When the first one showed at her door with stubble and a firm handshake, the plan changed.

There's no way a dude like that was sharing an apartment with her.

The only person she's sharing a wall with is me.

Not so I can picture what she's doing in bed on the other side, or offer to join in, but so that her impulsivity doesn't dig her holes she can't get out of.

On my way out after my visit, the retirement home passes me a folder with copies of the hospital bills.

There're a lot of zeroes for her care.

It's easy to think that girl problems are the only thing on my plate, but they're not.

Not by a long shot.

BROOKE

"We could have hired movers," I call after my brother as he and Rookie carry my dresser down the hall.

"No way. This is what family's for," he grits out.

"This is what subcontracting is for. You're too stubborn." I smile sweetly.

He sets down the furniture, wiping his brow as he grins back. "Runs in the family."

Most of my stuff is in a storage locker. I'm bringing only what I need, which is still several loads of clothes and shoes, boxes of makeup, a huge dresser and a blue chaise longue.

In the two days since Miles asked me to move in, I realized his place is actually perfect.

Though I'll never admit it, he was right about Hunter. The guy hit on me when he followed up. That wasn't going to work out.

Bottom line: rent is going up and I need a place. If being able to call my own shots in life and not have to pretend to be someone else means crashing with my brother's too-sexy-for-his-own-good teammate for a little while?

It'll be worth it.

Plus, it's only for a few weeks.

I've decided that by January 1st, I'll have my future mapped out and be out of here. As much as I appreciate the save, I'm not about to go from depending on my mom for income to depending on a guy.

I'll have the side benefit of accomplishing another top-secret project: getting over the crush I've been harboring for Miles Garrett.

It started innocently enough in college but reared its horny, inconvenient head in Vail.

At least this problem is one I have a plan for.

Having slept in the Kappa house with a ton of roommates, I know firsthand there's nothing sexy about sharing kitchens, bathrooms, and bedrooms.

Living with him will be my version of exposure therapy. A few weeks of sharing the same space and any attraction will evaporate completely.

We knock on the door and it swings wide.

Miles stands in the doorway, feet wide and arms folded. "What is this?"

His hair is a mess, presumably from bed or his fingers. The baby-blue hoodie shoved high on his muscled forearms bears the logo of a basketball camp he and Jay both attended. His dark jeans are more Wrangler than designer, but the way they hug his hips and legs is goddamned elite.

"You said I could move in. I brought a few things."

His mouth falls open as he watches Jay and Rookie carry the dresser past him.

"You don't have to go through with this. This is way beyond the call of duty," my brother informs his teammate.

Miles doesn't respond immediately, still taking in everything I brought.

I pat his chest before heading inside to direct my brother and Rookie.

Half an hour later, my furniture is in place. The bedroom is nearly as large as my old primary.

Unpacking my clothes, I stumble upon another problem.

"Where are my shoes going?" I murmur to myself, a designer heel in each hand. The closet is nowhere near big enough for all of them.

For the first time, it's setting in that I gave up my apartment.

Since I was a kid, I've always had a special place for my shoes. I loved collecting and arranging sandals, wedges and boots by color and style. Touching them and trying them on and picking the perfect pair was a comfort as much as a thrill. They were my decoration and my armor.

Emotion rises up my throat, a lump that won't go away.

A hand finds my shoulder and I glance up. Miles gestures to me, and I follow him to his room and his closet.

"But this is your closet," I point out.

Except compared to the last time I was here, only half a dozen pairs of basketball shoes remain on the shelves. The rest are wide open and look freshly cleaned, not a speck of dirt or dust to be seen.

He holds out his palms. "You're more into shoes than I am. I want you to feel at home."

I pass him the shoes, and he sets them on the shelf one at a time.

I agreed to be his roommate because I needed a place and didn't want him to think I can't handle being around him, but since we talked, he's clearly spent time making space for me.

My body brushes the fabric of his Henley, which is the same blue as his eyes.

Exposure therapy, I remind myself. Miles Garrett is far from the perfect man. The more time I spend around him, the more I'll realize it could never work—that no matter how funny and caring and attractive he is in small doses, more than that is stifling.

I clear my throat. "Rent. I want to contribute."

He cocks his head. "It's a condo. I own it."

"Oh." The soft carpet feels decadent under my toes as I shift on my feet. "Mortgage?"

"It's paid off."

"Then utilities."

"Not necessary."

"Groceries?"

"I have a delivery service when I'm home and an account with them." He's laughing at me now. His eyes are dancing as though he has a front-row seat at a show he's been anticipating for ages.

"Netflix," I say at last, triumphant. "I'll pay for streaming."

Miles cocks his head. "That costs money?"

"No, they just have a deal where hot people watch unlimited documentaries and trash TV."

His slow grin is as bright as the sunlight streaming in the windows.

If I was waiting for the day Miles doesn't affect me, I'll have to keep waiting.

I leave my brother and Rookie to set up some stuff in my room as Miles shows me around.

"No soaker tub?" I ask when he shows me the bathroom across from my room. I'm joking, but I'm kind of bummed. There's no reason to be. The bathroom is beautiful, white marble and a huge glass shower.

"You can borrow mine. It's in the ensuite off my bedroom."

His room.

Where he dresses that outrageously ripped body for an athlete's day.

Where he climbs into bed to close those dancing blue eyes.

Where he strips down to nothing and—

"We're ordering pizza." My brother's voice cuts into the haze of attraction between Miles and me.

They go to the kitchen and argue over toppings.

I go back to my room and find Waffles on the bed. "Hey, buddy. We're going to be hanging out more."

The Frenchie makes a noise of protest.

"He's a bit territorial. This is his room."

I look up to see Miles in the doorway.

"I won't be here long. A few weeks. A month tops."

I pull out a Sharpie and the desk calendar I bought yesterday and return to the bed, taking a seat next to Waffles as I unwrap the paper.

"You opened that for one month?" Miles drops onto the bed at my side, reaching out absently to scratch Waffles's neck.

"It's all I need." I uncap my Sharpie.

First thing tomorrow, I'll get to work.

Miles swipes the calendar from my hands before I can write on it. "You've barely moved in and you're that eager to get rid of me?" He sounds less irritated than curious. "I could be the best roommate you've ever had."

My fingers brushing his as I take the calendar back. I ignore the little zing of electricity between us. "Doubtful."

I deliberately cross off today on the calendar, two wide strokes of marker.

"Come on. I'm tidy. Objectively good looking. Make a mean almond milk latte." He grins.

I have to focus on getting my life together and getting out of here.

"What happened between us was a one-time thing," I say, choosing my words as carefully as I'd choose an outfit for an important event.

I rise and set the calendar square on the top of the dresser.

"I mean, it was more than one—"

"One *night*." The distinction seems important as I spin to face him. "It's going to stay that way."

Miles shifts back onto his elbows. He holds my stare so long I think I'm going to catch on fire.

If there was any question in my mind about our chemistry, the heat in his eyes chases it away.

But our only real connection is his loyalty to my brother, not to me.

"Pizza's here!" the guys holler from the other room.

Miles rises and glances at the team photo on top of a box. He sets it on my desk before gesturing to the hallway, his face unreadable. "After you."

5

BROOKE

Going to a Kodiaks event. Text if you need me. Breakfast is in the fridge.

—M

*D*eciding not to fuck your roommate and actually following through are two different things.

Particularly when he has the audacity to not only bust into a girl's life, but her dreams.

Waffles was happy to see me this morning, escorting me to the kitchen with his furry little body and excited snuffs.

When I open the stainless-steel door, I spot French toast, which I used to order when Miles took me out and none of the sorority sisters were looking, and fruit.

I pull out the food and heat up the French toast.

My first and only priority is figuring out my new job so I can get on with my future life. But in the two days since I arrived, it's been killing me how sweet Miles Garrett is being about me moving in with him.

The concierge called me "Miss Ellis" before I had a chance to introduce myself.

"Mr. Garrett asked us to do everything possible to make you comfortable," he went on after taking me on a walk-through of the parking facilities, where I was given a spot next to Miles's Range Rover.

Later, dinner was waiting for me when I got back from my storage locker.

"Added you to my meal plan," Miles said when I asked him. "Didn't know exactly what you liked, so I got more of everything."

He even offered to show me around the gym downstairs. I told him I'd figure it out, if only for the self-preservation of not watching him sweat.

When he returned and hopped into the shower ninety minutes later, I cranked Chappell Roan to drown out the sound so I wouldn't picture him under the spray.

I've learned that even with the Kodiaks in

Denver, Miles is gone for much of the day. But when he's here, he's a sexy, six-four distraction—bumping into him in the kitchen, being the target of one of those cocky grins, or sitting next to him on the couch to watch TV sends my pulse scrambling.

Today while Miles is at practice, I'm planning to spend my day going through social media.

I try the espresso machine but end up backing away when it spits steam at me. Apparently it only responds to my roommate, who coaxed the most delicious latte from it the afternoon I moved in, complete with happy face art in the steamed almond milk.

Yesterday morning he made me another, this one with the shape of Waffles's face in it after I commented on how adorable he was.

Elite is right.

Already in a deficit this morning thanks to the lack of caffeine, I pull open my computer. I still have my too-old phone, and I'm dreading the day it decides not to start.

My following is solid. Because I don't post bullshit I don't believe in, I might grow more slowly than someone like Caroline, but my followers are loyal and I appreciate that I can have a genuine exchange with them about where I'm going, what I'm wearing, what I love and hate.

Elise's brand would have been a slam dunk, but there are others out there. I go through my saved posts of companies and products I love and use and start to make a list of prospects. Next, I create a spreadsheet of everyone I've done brand collaboration posts with in the past. Then, I pick the top five and reach out to all of them to see if we can work together again.

When I look up from my computer, it's nearly noon.

I put on Lululemons and head down to the beautiful gym for a run on the treadmill.

After, I shower in my own bathroom, which may not have a soaker tub but is otherwise perfect.

I rub my eyes and stifle a yawn as I step out.

I'm going to need a coffee this afternoon. It's not only the espresso machine's fault but also my body's for prioritizing high def imagery of me and Miles in his massive bed over quality sleep.

I pick out clothes, finishing my outfit with gold earrings that belonged to my grandmother, then head to Miles's closet for shoes.

It smells like him in here.

Not sweat or dirt, but clean and male.

My gaze drifts toward the bedroom, landing on his big bed, with the midnight-blue cover darker than his eyes.

I catch my lip between my teeth.

Deciding I have no interest in Miles Garrett is hard when I'm horny. I've been amped since our night together in Vail. Every moment keeps replaying in my mind without permission.

Not only how it looked to see every inch of muscle, his sparkling blue eyes blown with hunger, and the strained grin. But also the feel of his arm hair rubbing against my smooth skin. The scent of him, clean and male and a little wicked.

I cross to the bed and lie down on the duvet. I press his pillow to my nose and inhale.

The scent of him lights me up.

Maybe relieving the ache is a sensible first step. A side quest, even, before the main event of forgetting him completely.

My fingers brush my stomach where my shirt has risen up.

Then tip-toe down my waistband.

The first touch is torturous bliss.

Pleasure spirals through me, twining with a sharp need that has my calves flexing and my toes curling.

I haven't gotten myself off since I moved in out of

some stubborn sense of pride. Or worse, the idea that he'd hear me and think he was the inspiration.

Except there's no pretending I'm imagining someone other than Miles right now—not when I'm in his bed, when he's the only one I've been able to think of since before the retreat.

A sound from the doorway makes me jump. But it's only Waffles, his little head tilted in curiosity.

"Stand guard, okay? And whatever you do, don't tell him."

Can dogs feel pity? I swear it's either that or compassion on the dog's scrunched little face before he turns and trots away.

I close my eyes and instantly I'm picturing Miles's huge hands pinning my wrists over my head. His firm mouth on my throat, my breasts, my stomach. His fingers sliding up the insides of my slick thighs while he groans in my ear.

I touch my breasts with my other hand. They've always been sensitive but he was so damn good with them.

Pleasure wraps around me like a silk thread, tightening with every stroke.

The pillow rubs against my face. My earring presses into my skin, the friction with the fabric making it tug deliciously at my lobe.

The climax sneaks up on me and steals my breath.

When I'm finished, I'm alone.

Oblivious Miles 2, Sexually Frustrated Brooke 0.

The phone rings on the bed next to me.

Does this man have a sixth sense for when I'm thinking filthy thoughts about him?

It's not Miles, though.

"Jay said he can't come to my speech. Can you?" my mom says by way of a hello.

"When is it?" I straighten my clothes, hurrying as if my mother can see me getting myself off in the bed of a basketball player.

Which she'd hate.

Not that she begrudges my brother his career, but her standards for me are different. She'd want me to end up with some guy who wears a suit to work and has a Roman numeral after his last name.

"An hour. It's a campaign year, and I have some big contributions pending," she reminds me.

I don't want to go, but I agree. It's easier to go along with Mom, plus meeting people is always worthwhile. If I want to step up my influencer career, I need to network my butt off.

I go change. Pretending I'm not into my

roommate is over for the day. I'm off to play a different part.

The speech is at a beautiful library across town. My mom's aide shows me to a seat in the second row.

The idea of meeting some new contacts in a low-pressure environment slips out the window when I spot Caroline and Kevin a couple of empty seats down.

"This isn't my seat," I tell Mom's aide, the knot already starting between my shoulders.

She double-checks her iPad. "It is. She specifically requested you sit here."

Of course she did.

"It's so nice to see you." Caroline's smile is fake syrupy sweetness.

We swap cheek kisses. "Kevin," I say, trying not to sound as if each syllable is poisoned.

"Brooke." He says my name in a way that has the hairs on my neck lifting. If Caroline notices, she doesn't let on.

I settle into my seat, crossing my legs at the ankles to better resist the temptation to kick the chair in front of me. "I'm surprised to see you here."

"I moved from Connecticut to be with my *fiancé*." There's no missing the emphasis on the word, especially as she lowers her gaze to her huge diamond ring. "Since we're engaged, it seemed like time to make the change." She turns to smile at Kevin, but he's already talking to someone else.

There's no reason to feel bad for her. She got the gig I planned on. I wanted to be Elise's new spokesperson, but Caroline lied and twisted the truth in order to win.

The speech starts, a lecture from a local academic about investments in libraries.

"That photo you showed me of Kevin," I whisper to Caroline. "The one where Miles..." I wave to my face and her expression darkens.

"When did that happen?" I lower my voice further.

She sniffs. "Forget I mentioned it. When Kevin came to me back then, it was in confidence."

Someone in the front row turns to censure us. We sit in silence the rest of the speech, and I replay her words in my mind as I sneak covert looks at Kevin and Caroline together, how distracted she looks and how possessive she seems.

Were they together behind my back in college?

The idea occurred to me before, but I always brushed it off.

Maybe Miles knew. Not only about the drugs, but about the cheating.

He was looking out for me as a favor for my brother, but it seemed like an overreach that he hit Kevin.

I think again of the breakfast in the fridge, the effort Miles has gone to in order to help me.

Surely that's beyond the call of duty for a friend or teammate.

It's making my head pound.

"Are you missing an earring?"

The first thing my mom says to me after the speech isn't thank you, or even hello.

I feel my lobe and realize I'm one short. "Damn it."

"You know how important jewelry is," my mom is saying. "You would have been better not to wear any, but this makes you look careless."

I smile and take her arms in my hands, making her inhale with surprise.

"Thanks for reminding me what matters. I was more worried that Grandma gave me these earrings and apparently I've lost one."

I swallow down the emotion rising up my throat.

Around these sharks, it would be viewed as weakness.

I need to try something different.

As my gaze lands on a familiar face that smiles in recognition, I know exactly what.

"This place is impressive," Trev says when I let him in.

"Make yourself at home."

I run into my room and search through my bag for the dark plum lipstick that looks amazing with my skin.

"I'm glad we ran into each other," comes his voice from the other room. "It's been a minute."

"Years," I echo.

He looks different than when we used to hang out as seniors. His glasses are more stylish, and he's in a suit.

Trev was a fun distraction after everything that happened the summer of junior year. He didn't care about the gossip and never took things personally.

Which is why we hooked up more than a handful of times through the fall.

It was never serious, for either of us.

He's exactly what I need to get through this day and the fact that the only man I've slept with in way too long is my roommate, who I need to avoid at all costs.

Moments later, I hear voices.

Shit.

I go out into the living room to see Miles and the guy in a standoff.

It's almost comical given Trev's the same height as me. Still, he played rugby in college, and from the way he fills out a suit, I'd bet he kept up the workouts.

"Trev, this is my roommate, Miles."

"Hope this isn't weird, but I'm a huge fan," Trev says.

Seriously?

"I'll be right there," I say, pasting on a smile.

I go back to my room and search through my bag of toiletries. There's a box of condoms, which I need. The voices outside—Miles's smooth one and Trev's excited one—set me on edge. *What are they talking about?*

The box feels suspiciously light.

I work it open only to find it empty.

Perfect.

"I have a question." Miles's voice rumbles from the doorway.

I straighten and turn, the empty box clutched in my hand. "Okay."

"Were you in my room earlier?"

I hope to hell I don't look guilty. I feel guilty, looking up at him.

"Yes," I say slowly. "To get my shoes."

It's not a lie. It's an incomplete truth.

He's got one brow raised, attention moving between the floor and my face. "That's all."

My heart skips. "What else would it be?"

It feels like a standoff. There's no reason he would suspect that I got off in his bed.

Partly because it's a little unhinged.

But more importantly, there's no evidence.

His gaze drops to the box in my hand and stays there.

"So you're going on a date?" he asks at last.

I'm off the hook. My shoulders relax. "Trev is an old friend I ran into at this event my Mom wanted me to go to."

"I could've gone with you if you needed someone."

Surprise has my brows shooting up. "It was a last minute thing. But thank you."

He nods.

"You're leaving for a road trip, right?" I hear myself say. "I can watch Waffles. Walk him and feed him and everything. It's the least I can do."

"Thanks." Miles starts to turn away, but stops. "You planning to bring him back here?"

"Waffles?" I'm confused.

"No. That guy."

"Oh. Maybe." I lift a shoulder. "Do you have any condoms? Apparently I'm out."

His brows knit together. He's fighting with himself. It's clear on every inch of his face.

"You don't want to do that."

I laugh. "Or what?"

"It wasn't a threat. I meant what I said, Princess —he's not what you want."

Miles thinks I want him? The arrogance is getting out of control.

"What happened to 'I'll be the best roommate you ever had'?" I challenge.

"I want you to feel safe and secure," he clarifies. "You don't like the food, say the word and I'll have it changed. If you hate your parking spot, pick one out and it's yours. I don't mean that I'm going to watch you fuck some guy who doesn't know what you need."

My heart is thudding against my ribs at his audacity, and the implication that Miles *does* know what I need. "So you're going to let a woman go on a date without protection."

His nostrils flare.

Finally, Miles disappears in the hallway, returning a moment later.

He presses something into my hand. I feel the smooth packet against my palm.

"This is yours."

He turns for the door, knocking the calendar on my dresser.

"One condom?" I say under my breath. "Is there a global latex shortage?"

"It'll be enough," he tosses over a shoulder. "We both know you won't be thinking of him anyway."

I open my fist and see the XL condom. But it's the glint of gold next to the packet that has the breath sticking in my chest.

It's my missing earring.

The one I left in his bed.

6

BROOKE

I never used to think about how funny a guy was before I went out with him. Humor was something I took for granted. But as I sit across from Trev, who's regaling me with stories about great things he's done, I resist the urge to yawn.

"Hey, Brooke. You still with me?" Trev's voice has me snapping back.

"Sorry. Didn't sleep much last night."

"Your roommate keeping you up?" he says with a knowing grin.

My water goes down wrong, and I reach for my wine to wash it down.

"I've heard those Kodiaks like to party."

I shrug. "In the summer, sure. But during basketball season, they're working their asses off."

"Not all of them. Miles has a reputation."

I set my wine back down, the base clinking against my plate. "I didn't realize you knew him."

Trev blinks in surprise. "Not personally."

"So, you don't know what he gets up to."

The implication that Miles is flaky irritates me. I've seen how devoted he is to family and friends, even to his game.

The problem isn't that I can't prove he's wrong—it's that I want to.

"Enough about them. We could go back to my place?" Trev suggests with a grin, reaching for the bill.

I lift a shoulder. "I should check on Waffles. I promised I'd watch him while my roommate was gone."

"Then we can go back to yours."

I chew my lip. "He doesn't love strangers."

Trev turns to face me. "You don't want to go home with me. It's cool."

I press my hands to my eyes. I'm not apologizing, because it's messed up for a woman to apologize to a guy for not fucking him, but this still feels awkward.

"I get that it was kind of our thing. And to be honest, I was thinking about it when you asked me out."

He cocks his head, looking genuinely curious. "So what changed?"

"Nothing you did. My mind is somewhere else. But I did have a good time."

Trev leans back and nods. "Yeah. Sure."

We leave the restaurant and take his car back to my place.

He drops me off, leaning in to kiss me.

I let him do it. A test to see if the connection can help.

"You won't be thinking of him." Miles's words come back.

Damn if he isn't right.

On the way home, I stop at a café for an almond milk latte to go.

A few weeks ago, I was living in my apartment, zero cares in the world. Now, I'm a lot more aware of things.

How much my life cost.

How much I focused on keeping up appearances.

How much I want my brother's teammate, even when I don't want to.

It's impossible to forget how sleeping with him felt. More than that, his kindness in looking out for me—without any real return—affects me.

71

With my mom, there was a specific payback: her career and her image.

With Miles, I get that he's helping Jay. But while maybe he was helping out his friend's little sister with Kevin years ago, or in Vail... Miles didn't need to move me in with him. He made his life harder by doing it.

I head upstairs to the condo, sipping the latte and grimacing. Definitely not elite.

"Miles?" I call tentatively when I step inside.

There's no answer. He already left.

The anticipation in my stomach evaporates along with the nerves.

I step out of my shoes and trudge across the living room. The soft wool of the carpet makes me curl my toes.

I set the latte on the coffee table and drop onto the couch, kicking my feet up on the end. There's plenty of reality TV to watch. I could call Nova or Ruby, or swing by the bar to see Sierra.

"It's you and me, buddy," I say to Waffles.

He snorts his agreement.

I should be overjoyed about having the place to myself.

I will be, I decide.

MILES

"Tapping out?" Clay asks from above me.

"No way." Sweat rolls down my face, and I press the bar overhead to finish my set.

The new guys work hard. The starters work even harder.

"Hawkins put up thirty-five points for Boston last night." I sit up and grab a towel.

Clay nods. "Plus ten rebounds and eight assists."

The fact that our all-star knows the guy's stats makes me blink. "You don't take anything for granted, do you?"

"Can't. That's the day you lose it."

I've got to ride my championship to bigger and better things.

If the team does well again this year—like conference finals well—it'll be a welcome boost for my career.

Grams needs a new retirement home. I decided that after the hospital. The ones I've called aren't cheap either, but I won't have her worry about it for a second. I'll do whatever it takes, even hire her a full-time support worker, to have her feel cared for. She deserves every ounce of comfort and dignity available.

"Jay's worried about Boston."

"Seems like they're his LA," Clay responds, referring to the team he spent time with that became his biggest rivals. "You know what's behind that?"

I twist the towel in my hands, considering. "Hawkins always got under his skin. Far as I know, they never played together. Probably just a beef that started with him talking shit."

"Dragon will keep you up at night until you slay it."

"What if you don't?"

He stretches both arms overhead, miles of black ink snaking across every inch. "Man can only go without sleep for so long before it fucks you up forever."

I turn that over. "How's Nova?" I ask, my attention settling on the ring tattooed on his finger.

"She's got some new pieces she's working on. Plus a show coming up." He's proud of her, and it's obvious from the way he talks.

"I'm happy for you, man."

Clay stretches an arm across his chest. "When you find the one, she's it. You wonder how you spent all the days before you were thinking about her."

He sounds like a guy who knows what he's talking about.

Since Brooke moved in, it's been... interesting.

She's everywhere. Eating my food, smelling like heaven.

She owns a fascinating volume of clothes, which appear to spill out of her wardrobe and into her room whenever I catch a glimpse inside.

Whether she's watching TV or drinking a coffee or researching on her computer, it's with single-minded focus.

When she turns that attention on me, it's like a drug. Every time we pass each other in a room, it takes all my restraint not to reach out and touch her.

Having her close was supposed to be a way to keep an eye on her, except all can think about is her.

I can't have her, not only because Jay would murder me.

Having a pro career and a healthy relationship aren't usually compatible. The Kodiaks come first for as long as I'm lucky enough to put on a uniform and take the court every night.

And there's no way I'm starting something unhealthy with Brooke Ellis.

She deserves more than that. She deserves everything.

When I went to bed the night before we left for the road trip, I tossed and turned, imagining her tangled in her sheets on the other side of the wall.

I wanted to do exactly what I was preventing any other man from doing—padding down the hall into her room, skimming my lips across her smooth throat, making her moan my name while I worked a hand between her thighs.

Shoving down every instinct was working until I found her earring in my bed.

As much as the idea that Brooke put it between my sheets for me to find turns me on, the possibility she didn't intend for me to know is even more torturous.

She was in my bed. On it, anyway.

The scent of her shower gel lingered on my pillow.

Now she's on a date with some asshole.

I wanted to drag him out of my condo by the hair, but I'm trying not to be that guy.

What was I supposed to do—lock the door with my teammate's little sister inside? Tell her the only man she's going to fuck is me?

Clay continues in the same breath, "I heard you got a new roommate."

News travels fast.

"I'm helping out a friend."

"Your friend a vampire? Because it looks like something's sucking the life out of you."

I laugh. I can't stop.

"What?" Clay grunts.

"Didn't know you were funny, man." The laughter fades. "But for real, I wouldn't do that to the team. I know we've got to focus."

We have to win here. They need it and I need it —for my Grams and my career.

7

Miles: How was the date last night?

Brooke: Fantastic. Your game?

Miles: Got a win. Tonight is another story. Back-to-backs suck.

Brooke: You need a lucky charm.

Miles: If I'm at home, I rub Waffles's ears before the game. Is he behaving himself?

Brooke: Perfect gentleman.

Brooke: Speaking of which, I figured out what happened with the earring.

Miles: You did.

Brooke: It must have fallen off. Waffles probably grabbed it and left it in your bed for you to find.

Miles: That would explain it.

Brooke: Totally. I'll be more careful about leaving things lying around. I'd hate for him to swallow something.

Miles: One problem with that theory, Princess.

Brooke: What?

Miles: Waffles can't jump that high.

8

BROOKE

The collaboration post of Caroline wearing Elise's new collection is a punch in the stomach.

It doesn't lessen as I flip through the slideshow of images.

This could have been the next step in my career.

Waffles whines up at me, and I tear my gaze away from my phone.

"You look like you could use a treat." He drops his butt to the carpet in an aggressively quick sit, his stump of a tail wagging.

Waffles is a particular dog.

He loves belly rubs and bananas.

He hates getting up early and when Miles leaves.

Yesterday, he helped me with work. By "help," I mean lay at my feet while I filtered through the responses to my brand partner follow-ups at Miles's dining table.

I also reached out to some high-profile brands. Most haven't responded, but a couple have.

What they're offering would barely pay for Waffles's dinner not to mention mine.

"Actually, I think we could both use a treat," I decide, reaching for my sneakers and grabbing Waffles's harness and leash.

We stop by a local café where I get a latte and a dog biscuit.

Jay and I never had pets growing up, but I can see the appeal. A dog doesn't care if you look perfect or have a weak moment. He just loves that you want to spend time with him.

It's oddly wholesome and heartwarming.

The morning light is soft and filtered. On impulse, I take a few pics of me, Waffles, the café and then post them as a slideshow.

When we get back, I'll cross off another day off the calendar with a big X.

I've been here a week yet I haven't cracked my career issues yet. Unless you're a Kardashian, there are only so many examples of women making it big as influencers—especially while keeping their integrity intact.

We're barely in the door at Miles's when the ding on my phone makes Waffles look up at the same time I do.

Collaboration inquiry reads the subject line.

I click into the message and my breath catches.

Vivaro. The company name sounds familiar. I cross to my bed, sinking onto it as I flip over to their social media.

Founded three years ago but growing fast. They make athleisure and are expanding to intimates.

I navigate through their latest collections, impressed.

"Cute, right?" I hold out the screen to Waffles, as if he can see what's on it. He gives a little grunt I take as approval.

They're looking for partnerships to launch their new collection and thought I would be a good fit. I can see why—my audience lines up with their perfectly.

"This could be exactly what we need," I say aloud. I type out a response to the message, asking if they'd send me a few pieces to try and providing my address.

Then I hoist the dog up in my arms with a whoop of triumph. He snuffles back joyously.

Now that my face is close to him, there's a lingering smell that makes my nose wrinkle.

"When was the last time you had a bath?"

I put on Lizzo and roll up my sleeves, waving for Waffles to follow me into my bathroom. I lift him into my shower, but he doesn't like that, pawing at the sides. So on impulse, I take him into Miles's soaker tub.

On the way, I pass his bed.

Embarrassment rises up at the vivid memory of me opening my hand and realizing he found my earring between his sheets.

Nothing says "I'm over fucking my roommate" like leaving jewelry in his bed while you were rubbing one out.

God. He probably thinks I'm so into him.

Waffles doesn't try to escape, and I'm able to clean him with the detachable shower head and Miles's shower gel.

By the time I'm done, Lizzo's halfway through her album and Waffles is shiny and smells like Miles.

I go to the hall closet to search for towels. Inside, I find towels—but also a box of photos.

Privacy says I shouldn't look. Still, Miles said I

could keep my shoes in his closet, so he's obviously not a stickler for personal space.

When I flip through the pictures, my lips curve without permission.

There are pictures of Miles playing basketball as a child and again as a teen after a growth spurt. His blue eyes shine, his grin wide and genuine. Photos of him with various teams. Winning in high school. With a younger version of his grams. With someone who must be his mom.

In each of them, he's with other people. He's popular because he's a good guy, a good friend. Not only with me, with everyone.

Waffles interrupts my thinking with a snuffling sound from the tub.

I quickly tuck the photos back in the closet and return to him, towel in hand.

"There you go, buddy." I dry him before I catch sight of my reflection in the mirror. He's sparkling clean, but I'm a mess.

My attention lands on the jacuzzi tub and longing rises up.

Ten minutes later, I've cranked the speaker on my phone and set it on the corner of the tub, and I'm sinking into a pool of bubbles. I sing loudly, my feet sticking out of the corner of the tub and resting on the edge.

Should have done this sooner.

Waffles comes up, setting both front paws on the side of the tub, and snuffles at me with curiosity.

"Damn, you're cute. Like your owner."

I can't resist lifting my phone with bubble-covered hands and taking a picture of his adorable face. I type out a text along with the image and hit Send.

MILES

"What do you want for Christmas?" one of our bench guys asks Rookie.

"Get him a clue," Atlas says, laughing. "You see the way he missed that pass? Hit you clean in the head. It's the meme that keeps on giving."

Rookie slaps Atlas's shoulder with a towel on the way past. "Least I'm on the court."

"Hey, everyone get your heads in the game," Jay hollers across the visitors' changeroom, and the guys settle down.

Miami made it deep into the playoffs last year. Next to Boston, they're our biggest rival in the East.

On the way over from the hotel with Jay, I glanced up at a screen to see that the oddsmakers have us picked to lose.

"We need this," he said to me.

"We'll get it." I said it with more confidence than I felt.

Road games are a physical and mental grind. We're also a week out from Christmas, and focusing on basketball is a struggle.

Brooke: Here's some luck for your road trip.

The text comes through when I'm headed to the arena.

The first thing I see in the photo is Waffles, his familiar face and cute ears.

That's when I realize he's perched on the edge of my bathtub, which is full of bubbles.

Brooke's painted toenails are sticking out. I trace it up her curved calves to her thighs.

She makes it sound as though the text is a peace offering. It doesn't feel peaceful. It feels like a fucking Trojan horse taking me apart from the inside out.

I'm about to shove the picture away when something new catches my attention and I do a double take.

In the mirror over the vanity in the corner of the photo, I can see Brooke's reflection.

Her lowered lashes and parted lips.

Her hair pinned up around her head.

Her round breasts halfway out of the bubbles as she poses to take the picture.

Heat shoots straight down my spine toward my dick.

She wanted me to see this. The realization makes me swallow.

I would've sworn there was nothing worse than watching her walk out the door with some other guy when I knew he couldn't be what she needed.

Now, I'm picturing her walking in on my shower to join me, or asking me to be her personal photographer for a private clothing-optional shoot—thoughts that take up at least half my focus when I'm joking with Rookie on the plane, or lifting with Clay, or running drills with Jay.

Since she moved in, we've both been dancing

around what happened. I've tried to be a good guy, but in my mind, being the best roommate she's ever had should have less to do with keeping dishes out of the sink and more to do with giving her multiple orgasms every night.

Miles: Leave any more clothing in my bed?

I shouldn't say it but can't resist.
Not when she's the one who upped the ante.

Brooke: Earrings aren't clothing. They're jewelry.

Miles: My bad. Leave any more jewelry in my bed?

Brooke: Like what, a nipple ring?

Fuck me.

The idea of her with one or both of her perfect tits pierced ruins any hope of focusing on the game.

I have to keep my head on straight. We're playing a strong Miami team in their arena.

Since I was a kid, I've always been competitive. I'm always the first one cracking a joke, or laughing at one, the first person to do a dare, the first to lay down a challenge.

Between the pressure on the court and everything else, my fingers dash out a text and hit send.

Miles: We get the win tonight, I want the rest of the picture.

It's a mistake.

I know it the moment I type it out, but it's too late to take back.

Every second that ticks by, I'm holding my breath.

Brooke: Miami's won five straight.

The knot in my gut releases, apprehension replaced with adrenaline.

Miles: So you don't have anything to worry about.

Brooke: Fine. Deal.

From the opening tip-off, it's a battle. The fans

are like a sixth player, giving us a grief on every foul shot and out-of-bounds.

I keep grinding.

"Come on, man. You got this." Jay slaps my back in encouragement.

My shots start going in, and as I rack up points, I create more and more of my own offense.

Jay and I manage to connect for a couple of big plays. His relief is evident from the other side of the court.

When we win, the guys rush over to clap me on the back and whip me with their towels.

I grab my phone and take a screenshot of the scoreline, sending it off to Brooke in a text.

Just in case she didn't see it herself.

When the interviewer grabs me for a post-game chat on the court, she says, "Gritty win tonight. What do we owe this new, tougher Miles to?"

"Trying to get wins while we're shorthanded." I'm still catching my breath.

"Rumor has it you're one of the most popular players in the league," the interviewer says with a laugh.

"If you can't make friends here, you're doing it wrong."

Tonight, I backed my team up big time. There's

no arguing with it. When I play like that, I'm worth every one of the millions of dollars I'm set to make this year.

"What's next for Miles?" she asks.

I'm riding a high of invincibility as I stare straight into the camera.

"I'm going home to collect."

9

BROOKE

"You didn't have to come early!" Nova throws out her arms to me as the door swings wide when I arrive.

"I didn't come to help. I came to drink your wine."

And possibly to avoid being home and running into my tall, gorgeous roommate who's supposed to get back any minute from his road trip.

Nova's sister, Mari, is queen of parties. Tonight is supposed to be a low-key celebration of Clay and Nova's new house.

The huge estate house is already decorated for the upcoming holiday. It's six bedrooms with even more bathrooms. Nova grew up on the road, so she never takes for granted having a place to put down roots and host friends and family.

"You look incredible," she says as she shows me some of the improvements they've made in their kitchen.

"Thanks." I glance down at my short black dress and suede booties. "I got a few pieces to try from this brand *Vivaro*."

"Oooh. They made the dress?"

"They made what's underneath."

I turn and unzip the back so she can see the aqua bra underneath from the box of products arrived this morning.

I remember how it looked when I put it on earlier and inspected the results in the mirror. I tamed my curls to add to the sleek look. "I need to take it for a full test drive before I commit."

"It's hot. What else did they send?"

"Two sets of workout bras and tights. I wasn't going to wear cropped leggings to your party, so here we are."

"If you do agree to work with them, you'll need a photographer. I'm officially offering my services."

"You're a lifesaver! And you do have the best eye."

"Pink?" a low voice calls from the door.

"In here!" Nova replies.

Clay appears from the hallway as I zip my dress back up. To his credit he doesn't look too disappointed when he clocks that I'm here. "Thought company wasn't coming for another hour."

"Come on. I'm not company." I wave a hand.

"Good. Then I can ask you to leave and come back when I'm done with my wife."

Nova laughs. "That can wait."

"Not what you said on the phone last night." He crosses to his wife and brushes a kiss across her lips.

Damn. They're so freaking cute it hurts to watch them.

When Clay pulls back, my friend is beaming. "How was the flight?"

"Rookie's been watching these animal tricks reels. We made him plug in his headphones, but now all we can hear is him laughing." Clay changes gears smoothly. "Miles had a good game."

I look between him and Nova. "Why are you telling me?"

"He's playing better than I've seen him play. Doesn't happen without making a change." He reaches for a water and grabs his bag to take upstairs.

The fact that Clay's here means Miles is getting home anytime.

I try to put it out of my head as we finish preparing.

An hour later, the open concept great room and kitchen is full of a couple dozen Kodiaks, family, and friends.

"The team is heading into the midseason tournament," Chloe's saying to me, Nova and Sierra. "It's good for the press and the fans to stay excited through the holidays. The winning team and players get a bonus."

"How are their chances?" Sierra asks.

"Better than they were a few weeks ago," Chloe admits. "Especially after last night."

My gaze drags toward the sound of the door just as Miles walks in.

He's in jeans and a blue button-down that matches his eyes and pulls across his broad shoulders and the muscles of his chest. His hair is styled straight up. I want to brush a hand across the top to see how it'd feel, or what he'd do if I did.

My brother comes in after him.

"The man of the hour!" Atlas calls, clapping Miles on the back.

It's a few minutes before Miles wanders over to our group, a beer in hand.

"Nice place." He looks around, admiring.

"Thanks, Miles." Nova's eyes soften.

"I remember how stressed Clay was before the wedding," Miles says. "Trying to get the perfect house."

"I can't imagine him doing that," Chloe says, shaking her head.

"I can," Sierra counters. "He bought half the bar to help out my dad. It's always the ones who act tough that have a soft heart underneath."

Miles and I share a smile.

"Brooke! You have to show the girls your *Vivaro*."

"Her what?" Sierra and Chloe chorus, exchanging a look.

"It's this line of sexy underwear Brooke's going to partner with."

I feel Miles's eyes on me.

"I've heard of them," Chloe says. "Don't they make yoga clothes?"

"They're branching out," I confirm.

"And they sent you free lingerie? Sweet, maybe I need to be an influencer," Sierra decides before Chloe asks her a question about how to mix a drink, and Nova's called away by her husband.

"So you're going to be a lingerie model now."

The teasing in Miles's voice makes me angle my head. "I haven't decided. You think I could hack it?"

His gaze skims down my figure. "I think you'd break the internet."

I love the way he looks at me. As if I'm at the center of every fantasy he's ever had.

My palms are sweating. I drop my clutch and when I bend to pick it up, something shiny falls out.

Miles beats me to retrieving it.

"You didn't use it." He holds up the foil packet with the letters XL printed on it, the wrapper glinting in the light.

I lift a shoulder.

Triumph etches on his face. I wait for him to give me shit, but all he says is, "I'm glad."

"Why?"

"You know why."

I laugh.

He's flirting with me. I like it.

It feels safer here somehow, surrounded by our friends.

Not like back at the condo we share where anything could happen.

"You still owe me the rest of that photo." His voice is lower now.

"There was no rest of the photo."

It's Miles's turn to chuckle. "For real? That was my entire motivation for winning. Guess I'll have to make do with what I saw in the mirror."

"The mirror," I echo, confused.

I reach for my phone and pull up the image.

I'd been so intent on Waffles's adorable face, I didn't realize I was giving Miles a lot more than I planned.

My teeth wrestle with my lip.

"Don't tell me that wasn't the idea." He arches a brow.

"It was all about the dog," I vow.

"Well, fuck." His laugh is fuller this time.

I promised we wouldn't do this if we moved in together. But damn, resisting him, resisting the pull between us, is taking everything in me.

"Maybe there's a consolation prize." I glance past him, then take his wrist and tug him after me into another room filled with easels and stacks of canvases and boxes.

The solarium is dark, lit only with soft fairy lights and the moonlight streaming in through the windows.

Music drifts in from the hallway, plus the sound

of our friends laughing. My senses are focused on Miles, and the heat flooding my body.

I want him more than I can remember wanting anything.

"Pop quiz. What's better than a picture, Garrett?"

I reach for his hand and press it between my legs under my skirt.

He stills, and the world seems to slow down, too.

For a guy who isn't known for his self-restraint, he's remarkably composed.

I wouldn't know how much he wanted me if it wasn't for the uneven rasp of his breathing. The way his fingers flex on my thigh rather than pulling away.

The tension between us grows until my chest is tight with it. Every part of me is vibrating.

"You sure?" Miles's voice is rough.

I nod.

He exhales on a groan.

Fuck it.

I can feel the moment he thinks it.

The next second he's crowding me, leaning in, his forehead pressed to mine while his fingers stroke up the inside of my thigh.

When he brushes over the thin satin, I moan.

It's the lightest damned touch but it feels so good.

My feet step wider apart, as far as the tight skirt will allow.

Still, his massive hand strokes the insides of both thighs every time he moves.

"This is the stuff you just got?" He presses against the fabric.

"Mhmm. I'm test driving it to see if I like it."

The rub of my panties as he drags them to one side with a finger has pleasure dancing along my nerve endings, chased with anticipation.

"If you need a second opinion…" His thumb strokes across my clit. "It feels fucking fantastic."

The smoldering desire catches fire and turns into a blaze.

Each slide of his skin over mine where I'm sensitive only makes me want more.

He presses one finger inside, and my head falls back against the wall. I grab his shoulder, my nails digging into the muscles through his shirt.

"That's it," he whispers. "Right there."

It's arrogant, the idea that one finger is enough to get me off, but the punch line is he's right. My body clenches around him.

When he eases another finger inside, I inhale sharply.

"Don't," I say.

"Don't what?"

"Don't go slow."

He drags my skirt up around my waist, hooking my leg around his hips. His lips crush down on mine.

Miles tastes like mint and the faintest hint of vodka. His huge body looms over me. His mouth is demanding.

We're both physical people, but there's a new intention to him, an intensity, that reminds me how he got to be in the one percent of human beings who make a living playing games with their bodies.

I arch into him and he drags me toward the climax I've been chasing.

I start to moan, and he claps a hand over my mouth. "Damn, I love feeling you come. But unless you want the entire house to hear you," he murmurs, and I can feel his smile against my throat, "be quiet about it."

His words and touch and voice send me over the edge.

Pleasure spirals through me, starting deep in my core. I'm shaking with it, every part of me greedy for more.

Miles holds me, coaxing sensation after sensation from my body until I sag against the wall.

He holds me up with an arm behind the small of

my back, leaning his forehead against mine as our heart rates recover.

"Can I see the rest of it?"

I have to blink to remember what he means. I reach up to the low neckline of the dress, tugging it down enough to expose the low demi-cups of my bra.

He rubs a hand across his jaw. "I hate it."

"What?!"

"Yeah. It's got to go." He glances over his shoulder before returning to me. "Meet me at the Range Rover in five."

It takes me a second to appreciate the hunger in his slow grin. "You want to leave?"

"I've been on the road all week and just carried five guys to a W against the top team in the league. There's only one thing I want to do."

"Sleep?"

He brushes a quick kiss across my mouth that's as hungry as it is gentle.

"Save my roommate from some bad lingerie."

10

MILES

"Can't believe you used your dog as an excuse," Brooke laughs as I swipe the keycard at the door.

"Think they suspected anything?"

"Nova did," she answers as we step inside.

Waffles yips at us.

When I got back from our road trip, I was disappointed she wasn't at the condo when I walked in.

All I could think about before was getting my hands on her. Back at Clay's in that dark room, it was just her and me and a pile of need that's been building up for what feels like a lifetime.

But now that we're here in this place where we're also roommates, it feels different.

"Want a drink?" I ask, already moving toward the kitchen. Familiar rhythms start to take over.

"Like a coffee?" She smiles.

"Told you my work was elite. But tonight, I was thinking something more grown up."

I pour us each a glass of whiskey, no ice. We stand in the kitchen, close enough to touch, but not touching.

Her clothing is tidily back in place, but her lips are swollen from mine.

Our eyes meet, and there's desire and anticipation mirrored back at me.

"Hi, Roomie," Brooke murmurs.

"Hi," I answer.

She pivots to face away from me, glancing over her shoulder. "You only a scorer or can I get an assist?"

I blink before realizing she wants help with her zipper.

The distance between us evaporates in a heartbeat. It's fine work with my big hands, but I'm tugging down, not hard enough to break the dress.

When it's all the way open, she pushes it down her hips and turns back around.

The bra, if you can call it that, is light blue. It cups her breasts and fits tightly down her ribs, ending above her navel. The matching thong rides high on her hips.

Fuck.

She's every wet dream I've ever had.

"Thought you said you hated it?" she prompts, teasing.

"It's got to go. But..."

"But?"

"Not yet."

And then we're kissing.

Our hands roam each other's bodies. Her tits fill my palms through the bra, her little moans making me harder than I've ever been.

"You're so fucking sexy," I say against her mouth.

We stumble to the couch and fumble with our clothes. She shoves impatiently at my shirt, trying to drag it over my head. I bend to help.

I'm desperate to feel every inch of her. I grab her ass in my hands, pulling back to admire the way her tits spill out of the fabric.

I shift her up on the arm of the sofa, stepping between her legs as she works off my jeans.

"Day you moved in, I took one look at your shoe collection and pictured all of it on my floor."

Her low laugh strokes down my spine. "Instead you put them in your closet. What a good boy."

My pants are gone, my shorts too. My cock hits my stomach as she shoves away the last of my clothing. Our breaths are ragged and heavy, the only sound in the room. Her lips cling to mine as if I'm all she needs.

I stroke up the inside of her thigh, my fingers pressing against the fabric of her thong. "You'll be calling me something else in a minute."

I slip a finger under the panel. She's soaking wet, and knowing how turned on she is only makes this hotter.

I lift her by her hips and carry her to my bedroom, hitting the dimmer on the way so we're not in darkness, because I sure as hell want to see what's about to happen.

I set her on the duvet and admire her. Her dark hair splays out in curls. Her skin glints softly in the low light. Her breasts are full and perky, her thighs curved and strong.

"Have I told you that your tits are impeccable?"

"I'd rather you showed me." She reaches behind her to unhook the bra, taking a moment because there must be a dozen hooks.

Then she tosses it off the bed.

"Fuck," I groan as I bend over her and lower my mouth to her breast.

She arches against me and I give it the attention it deserves before switching to the other side. I can't get enough of her, of the way she responds to me.

But it's not enough. There's so much more I want to give her, to show her.

I drag off her thong and part her legs. "Wider."

She hooks a hand around each knee and puts herself on display.

"Don't fucking move." I press a hand against each of her thighs to hold her there as I bend over her.

I lick her, one slow stroke, then another, until she's writhing and moaning.

Brooke wraps her legs around me, then her lips are trailing down my chest, her tongue playing with my nipple. "I want you inside me."

I groan, my hands sliding up her thighs, feeling her heat.

I reach for the box of condoms on the table and retrieve one packet.

Brooke grabs the condom out of my hand, glancing at the label. "And here I figured you kept the XL ones purely to intimidate your roommate's dates."

I grin. "They're not just for show."

She rolls it on me, giving an extra squeeze at my base.

I grip her hips, pulling her down onto my cock. She gasps, her eyes widening in surprise at the feeling. When I thrust up into her, our bodies move together. Brooke moans, her head falling back, her hair cascading around her face.

My hands cup her face, and I kiss her. She responds, her hands gripping my biceps as we move together.

Our lips never leave each other. Sweat drips down our bodies as we move faster, our breathing ragged. Brooke's legs wrap around me, pulling me deeper into her.

I feel her tightening around me, her moans coming every time I sink inside her.

I thrust harder, my own release building.

It takes everything in me to slow down, to make my strokes more shallow.

"What are you doing?" she pants.

"Trying...to hold off..."

Her low chuckle reverberates through her, and me. "That's cute. How's that working out?"

My teeth grind together as her lips brush my chest.

I slide a hand between us and pinch her clit between my fingers. "You tell me."

She cries out. Then shudders around me as she reaches her climax.

Thank fuck.

I stroke into her deeper, harder, faster. My hips buck as I spill into her.

We collapse onto the bed, our hearts pounding. My body is still shaking, but a sense of peace and contentment settles over me. We lie there, sweaty and spent, our bodies entwined, the only sounds in the room our ragged breaths.

I get up long enough to toss the condom before sliding back into bed. Brooke starts to shift out the other side.

"Where are you going, Princess?" I grunt, not waiting for a response before I pull her close.

She squirms in protest. "You can't hold me hostage."

"You liked how I was holding you a second ago."

I feel her huff of breath as much as I hear it. "You're bossy as hell, Garrett."

I lock my arms around her and smile into her neck until I fall asleep.

11

BROOKE

*S*neaking out of your roommate's bed without waking him is harder than it sounds.

Especially when his massive arm is around you and his leg is pinning yours.

But after last time, being the person who trusted him only to wind up alone? I'm not about to do that again.

"Hey! I didn't know you were bringing a friend," Nova chirps when I arrive at the gallery where she's showing pieces. "Thought you only looked after Waffles when Miles was away?"

"I'm going for dogsitter of the year." I pass her a coffee.

She walks with me the length of the gallery

where her paintings are being hung for an event starting next week. Most are still covered.

"I knew it would be the perfect backdrop for our little photo shoot."

"And I'm grateful." I shrug out of my jacket, stripping down to the dark green longline bra and leggings. I didn't want to risk sticking around at home to do my hair, so I brought a few supplies and touch up my hair and makeup there.

"Maybe against the brick?" I gesture to the textured wall, painted white.

She does a few test shots on her phone and I put on music.

"Come on, let's sell some leggings," Nova says with a wide smile.

We start taking pictures. I channel my dance training, starting with elegant poses. Then I shift to more casual ones.

It's fun being in front of the camera, but even more, I love hanging out with my best friend.

Even Waffles gets in on the excitement. I pull him into one of the photos.

After a few more, I reach for the nearest painting and find the tape attaching the wrapping paper. "May I?" I ask my friend with a pleading look.

"I suppose."

I peel off the brown paper and reveal the painting, an abstract swirl of bright colors that bring to mind sunsets over the mountain. "This is incredible. It needs to be in the next one."

"You know you're glowing," Nova says after a few more shots.

"It's the light," I say.

"I think it has more to do with where you ran off to last night."

Guilt rises up. "Was it that obvious?"

"Only to me." She winks.

Ending up in bed with Miles again wasn't part of the plan. Seeing how much he wanted me after I'd accidentally sent him a sexy pic made it really hard to remember why we shouldn't.

The way he made me come in secret at Nova's made it even harder.

"I'm a little surprised he didn't want to come with you."

"Technically, he wasn't awake when I left."

"You snuck out." She gasps. "You ran away and took his dog with you—"

"Dogsitter," I remind her.

"Does Waffles deserve to be used as an excuse?"

The Frenchie hears his name and immediately

perks up, cocking his little head with a curious whine.

"Don't you guilt me too," I tell him before turning back to Nova. "It's not a big deal. We have chemistry. It boiled over. Again."

"What if it's more than that?"

I don't have an answer. I've never had someone go to so much effort, and trying to decide why is beyond me right now.

My gaze focuses on the painting once again. "Why isn't this on *your* social?"

"I haven't had a second. Since the wedding and moving into the new house, plus the start of the new season, we've been living in chaos."

We unwrap the rest of the paintings and I snap pictures with my phone. "Okay. You're going to post this one now and another tomorrow and this on the weekend. When does the show open?"

"Saturday."

"Hmm. No, let's do it this way." I explain my changes. "You'll have a line around the block."

"I'm not sure how to do that."

"Here. Give me your phone." I download a scheduling app and link it to her social, then I queue up the posts we talked about. "There. All you have to do is respond to the comments."

Nova claps her hands in excitement. "You're hired."

I laugh, retrieving my coffee from where I set it. "You know I'll help anytime. It's the least I can do for you helping with my little photoshoot."

"I'm serious, Brooke. This goes beyond the scope of a little photoshoot. Can I hire you?" The earnest hope on my friend's face makes me consider her request.

"What do you have coming up?"

She tells me what she'd like to do for the next few months.

"If I were you..." I flip over a napkin and mock up a quick content plan on the fly.

"That's perfect! I'll try it. Will you try something for me?"

I frown. "What's that?"

"Don't run away from Miles. Don't over analyze it or try to put a label on it or decide what it should be. Just have fun for a while."

MILES

"Tomorrow's home game marks the start of the midseason tournament. I've got two things to say heading in. First, props to Garrett," Coach says. "That was beast mode. Keep it up."

Guys clap me on the back.

"Second...we have an addition for practice today."

A cheer goes up as Atlas comes around the corner and pulls off his hoodie.

"Nice of you to finally join us," Jay says with a grin of relief.

If there's one thing our title last year taught us, it's that once you win, you have to keep winning.

I wish I could say my only distraction is Grams. Of the facilities that have gotten back to me about Grams, the best one is crazy expensive. I sent a note to my accountant to ask how many years I can afford to keep her there. Yeah I make bank today, but you never know how soon a career could end.

But it's more than that.

Last night at the party, my roommate gave me one "fuck me" look and my control evaporated.

I'm used to women hitting on me but it wasn't just any woman.

The second she took my hand and led me to that room, I couldn't pretend to be immune.

Hooking up with her in Vail was hot.

But making her come in my bed with my name on her lips was an experience I'll never forget.

Problem is, I'm craving more than one night.

Especially after waking up without her this morning.

I should be grateful she didn't try to make this into something it can't be.

I don't share my bed with women. I'm chill about a lot of things but where I put my head down is my own place. So, it's hard to put my finger on why this is bugging me so much.

My phone rings and I grab it without looking at the call display.

"Yeah?" I say into the handset.

"Garrett. Hope you're sitting down."

It's my agent. We don't talk much except leading up to contract years.

"What is it?"

"There's a deal on the horizon. A shoe sponsorship."

I blink. "You sure you called the right number."

I'm the guy everyone goes to for help planning a party or pulling a prank.

I'm not the shoe deal kind of guy.

He barks out a laugh. "You're in the running but they want to see more before making a decision."

"How much?"

"Not confirmed but it's out there." He names a figure that has my jaw going slack.

It's almost as much as my entire contract. It would make a difference in my Grams's life, ensuring sure I could provide for her as long as she needs it.

"Their brand is wholesome. They want someone everyone's talking about, but they've had their eye on you for a while."

"What do I need to do?"

"Easy. Keep playing the best ball of your life and don't let anything distract you."

I'm still turning over the potential shoe sponsorship when I get up to my place.

Even though my year's been strong so far, it's not obvious why they picked me over the hundreds of other guys.

But every thought evaporates when the door swings wide before I can turn the handle.

"There you are!" Brooke hovers in the doorway.

She's wearing these green leggings and a matching top with a Kodiaks zippered sweatshirt over top. Her face is perfectly made up, her hair pulled back in a high ponytail. Waffles pokes his head between her feet, a purple bandana around his neck.

When he sees me, he dashes over, a squirming ball of energy and happy yips.

My bag lands on the floor as I bend down to scratch his ears, which I swear are softer than usual.

"That smell…" It's heaven. Cinnamon and sugar.

"I baked. You like cinnamon rolls?"

Fuck me.

I didn't expect to be greeted by some kind of cheerleader-with-a-spatula fantasy.

I grab my bag and take it inside, letting the door click after me.

Brooke heads back into the kitchen and bends to open the oven. Her ass looks so fucking good in those leggings that it's all I can do not to drag her against me right this second.

"New outfit?"

Let everything in the oven burn. I'll eat the charred remains with a grin.

"It's from the same company that offered me a collaboration. Nova and I were down at a gallery putting some shots together for a post."

She sets a plate with one sticky bun on it front of me. It's a work of art, the glaze glistening on top.

My stomach growls and I rip off a piece of the pastry and devour it. My tastebuds sing.

Fuck, that's good.

I peel off a piece and hold it out.

She goes to take it, but I shake her off until she opens her mouth.

I pop it in. Her lips brush my fingers and my dick jumps a mile.

Brooke looks surprised but reaches for her phone, turning up the cracked screen.

"Still haven't gotten a new one?"

"Got other things on my mind."

She flips through photos and holds one up.

In it, she's posing with one leg extended out behind her and one hand above her head. The light streams in from a window, shining on her golden skin.

I swipe through, and each one's better than the last.

Then another where she's laughing.

A third that's a selfie with her and Nova, and they're both grinning and unselfconscious.

"Whatever they're paying you, Princess, it's not enough."

I tear off another piece of the cinnamon bun and eat it. *Goddamn.*

"If this is a thank you for the sex, I'm impressed," I say when I'm finished.

"It's a thank you for the room. And the elite coffee. And generally being so nice to me," she corrects.

"So...the thank you for the sex is still coming?"

It's throwing me that she hasn't acknowledged what went down, especially since we've been dancing around our chemistry since the second she moved in.

Brooke serves me side-eye as she sets her phone down on the kitchen table. "You can't seriously expect a woman to thank you for sex."

"I never expect a thank you. But I do appreciate one, especially if she comes as many times as I made you come last night."

"Maybe I made myself come and you were just an attractive accessory."

It knocks the wind out of me a little. I recover.

"Your new favorite."

"Excuse me?"

"Judging by how much you screamed, my tongue is your new favorite accessory."

She rolls her eyes.

"You were gone when I woke up," I point out.

She doesn't react until she's done her bite. "We were scratching an itch, not pledging our undying love."

She's trying to draw boundaries. If I had my head on straight, I'd do the same.

"How was practice?" she asks.

Hello, hard left turn.

Apparently, I'm the only one ready to admit our connection is legendary.

I can play that game with her. It's not so different from basketball. You get in close with someone, there's finesse involved.

"I'm up for this shoe contract. It's a huge deal that would help cover Grams's care for years."

"What's the brand?"

I tell her, and she looks it up. Her brows pull together in concentration as she bends over the phone.

"It would be a great fit." Brooke's gaze lifts to mine, delight taking over her expression.

"I don't know. I'm Miss Congeniality. Most likeable. Best prankster. Best smile. The last one was from *Cosmopolitan*," I add helpfully.

Her eyes narrow. "There's more to you than that. You care about people. I don't even know if you realize how much because you cover it up with jokes. But you're a good person. A good player, but more than that, a good man."

Well, fuck.

My plans for keeping this thing between us locked down didn't account for her backhanded compliments.

She tugs away to cross to a whiteboard I didn't notice in the corner of the living room.

That's new.

She makes notes with a marker in a scribble I can barely read, checking her phone for details in between.

"Looks like you're drawing up a play," I say, chuckling.

"I am. A strategy for how to get you that endorsement deal. I can help you shape your image so you can get the campaign. You'll be the *perfect* spokesman."

I've been around women who wanted what I was and what I could do for them—never someone who saw the man I *could* be, who wanted me to be my best.

I close the distance between us, coming up behind her.

She stills. "What's wrong?"

I push her ponytail to the side and brush my lips over her neck.

"Can you focus for a second, Garrett? I'm trying to help you," she murmurs. Her body betrays her as she arches toward me.

"Something more urgent I could use a hand with." I wrap one arm around her shoulders and pull her back against my chest.

My agent said no distractions, but this doesn't count.

One, because we're literally working on the deal.

Two... if there's a straight man who can resist Brooke Ellis, I'd love to meet him.

I want her.

Badly enough that I don't know what I'm going to do if she says no.

Crawl into a ball in my bed and howl like an animal.

The thought has my teeth grazing her skin. Her breath hitches.

"Typical."

But she runs a palm down my abs to where I'm already hard.

Hallelujah.

"You want me to fuck you before we talk about this deal?" I ask as I spin her around. "Or after?"

She grabs my neck for balance, her eyes bright with arousal and challenge. "After."

I hitch her legs up around my waist, knocking the whiteboard over. "Too late."

I carry her to my bedroom.

It turns out that howling isn't so bad when you're not doing it alone.

Shorthanded Kodiaks Open Midseason Tournament With A Bang: Bears Crush OKC

Dallas Blindsided by a Surging Kodiaks Squad in Second Round

Kodiaks Claim Three Straight Wins: Garrett a Midseason Revelation

BROOKE

"*D*id you see HoopsNews eat their words?"

My brother hollers loud enough the entire table can hear him over the music and laughter that fill the bar.

"It's the media's job to make news," I remind him, nudging him with an elbow.

He snorts. "They're sure as hell doing it."

The team and friends are at Mile High following the third win of the midseason tournament. I'm seated on the outside next to my brother and Atlas. Clay, Nova, and Rookie are on the far side.

In mid-December, there are more purple Kodiak hoodies and hats on fans in the streets than holiday clothing. The entire city is swept up in

Kodiaks fever after a lull that feels like it's lasted far too long.

"You're going to Mom's for Christmas Eve," Jay says, but it's a question.

"That's the plan. Why?"

"I saw her the other day and she said she wasn't sure."

I roll my eyes. "She asked me to help with an appearance last week and I said I was busy. She's not used to hearing no."

Jay cocks his head. "Busy with what?"

"You kidding? Campaign is my new wallpaper," Rookie says, nodding to me.

I laugh.

"What campaign?" my brother asks.

"It's not a campaign. Just a post I did with this activewear brand."

Rookie's already holding out his phone to my brother.

Jay's brows lift. "Mom seen this?"

I smack his shoulder. "I'm grown and they're called leggings and a sports bra."

"Amen," agrees Rookie.

The post I made for *Vivaro* including pics from my mini photo shoot with Nova was a hit.

This morning I got an email from their head of

partnerships saying how much they loved it and want to do more together.

It's almost enough that I can tune out the haters that jump in with their judgments about my body, their criticisms about what I'm wearing.

I try to skim over them, to imagine they're talking about someone else. Or remind myself they don't know me and that I'm the one getting paid.

"So, Christmas means a late night with the senator?" Atlas says from the other side of the booth.

"My mom will have one glass of her favorite wine and pass out by ten," I state, grateful to stay on the topic of holidays at my family's home.

"If you're smart, you'll all be asleep too with a game Christmas Day broadcast on every network," I point out.

It's a tradition that the top teams play on Christmas, and the Kodiaks being defending champs ensures it.

"It's against LA." Clay's across the booth, an arm draped around Nova.

"Which is Clayton Wade for 'don't lose,'" Sierra offers as she drops off fresh pints.

"You speak Kodiak very well," Nova jokes, and we all laugh.

LA was the team's prime competition from last

year, and Clay has an eternal chip on his shoulder when it comes to them.

"Good thing Garrett's playing like he's got a cheat code," Rookie says, looking up.

"Someone trying to jerk me off?" Miles slides in next to me. Four smaller people could fit without a problem. With three of the four being professional basketball players, it's a squeeze.

I feel every inch of him through our clothes.

"You assume every time you hear your name that it's a compliment?" I toss.

"Obviously." He grins in my direction.

He's dressed in jeans and a zip-up sweater. I'd know it without looking, because I had a hand fisted the fabric of each an hour ago when he parked the Range Rover in an underground lot nearby.

Every inch of me heats, and it takes a concerted effort not to bite my lip.

Does it look like we've been hooking up for the past week?

Because we totally have.

Since the night of Clay and Nova's party, every spare second that he hasn't been on the Kodiak clock and I haven't been working, we're fucking each other's brains out.

In his bed.

In my shower.

On the chaise longue.

If sex were a religion, we've been devout.

The man is a beast in bed. He's fun and creative and has zero judgment.

Each time we're together leaves me more convinced I want to keep riding the ride.

"It's because of Waffles. He's lucky for all of us," Damon decides.

"How do you figure?" I ask. "He's had Waffles for a few years."

Damon shrugs. "Got any other ideas?"

My gaze meets Miles's, his eyes dancing.

A slideshow of places we've hooked up flashes across my brain and I wonder if the same thing is happening for him.

"Guess not," I say into my drink, gulping like I've been walking in a desert all week.

"We're all having Christmas dinner with Kodiaks and fam after the game, right?" Rookie asks.

Harlan, the GM, is hosting an event for the team and family.

"Not me," Miles says, shaking his head. Groans go up from around the table.

"You too cool for us?" Damon challenges.

Miles shifts back, grinning. "I don't want to take

Grams out with her arm still healing. I'm taking over food and I'm going to spend it with her."

"That's really sweet," Nova sighs. There's murmured agreement and my heart kicks in my chest.

An hour later, Miles and I bump into each other as I'm coming out of the bathrooms and he's heading there.

"Garrett." My voice is rough, either from the alcohol or something else.

"Roomie." His brows lift, the corners of his mouth too. "You don't like me calling you 'Roomie,'" he teases.

His tone makes me frown. "I didn't say that."

"Didn't have to." He looks both ways before stepping closer, capturing my hands in his. His lips brush my cheek, trace my jaw. "I could call you Princess."

A shiver runs through me and I make a non-committal sound.

"I could call you mine." His teeth graze my throat and I *melt*.

The hooking up is addictive, but more than that, the crush I swore I'd get over isn't retreating—if anything, it's deepening.

Sneaking around is hot, but I can't pretend that

all I'm feeling is the thrill.

"There a reason Rookie keeps looking at you with dreamy eyes?" Miles murmurs.

"He saved my posts as his phone wallpaper."

"For real? Shit. Dude's got a hard screen coming in practice tomorrow."

His mouth brushes mine.

Surprise has my brows lifting.

Is Miles Garrett jealous?

He might've acted like it before, but this is the first time he's admitted as much.

I've never known my brother's friend to get jealous over a woman, or possessive.

The sound of laughter from around the corner jolts us both out of our haze.

"I'm glad someone likes the posts," I murmur.

I regret saying anything when Miles frowns. "What do you mean?"

"Just a lot of haters. It's fine. It happens with most posts, and it happens more to women who look like me."

He releases me with one hand to pull up the post on his phone. He reads, his mouth tightening the further he goes.

"This is bullshit."

His reaction triggers the cascade of thoughts I've been repeating to myself like mantras.

"Having dissenting views isn't strictly a bad thing. It helps the algorithm."

"Fuck the algorithm."

My lips curve at the way he defends me. "Fuck the algorithm," I agree.

"That's right. You're beautiful in and out of everything. If you forget, I'm going to remind you later. Repeatedly." Miles tugs on my hair before releasing me.

I watch him head into the bathroom, glancing back at me with a wink.

"See you later, Roomie."

"Something's wrong with my Instagram," Nova says as we walk down 16th Street.

"What is it?" I flip my collar, tugging it up around my face to keep the wind out.

It's a week before Christmas, and Nova and I are taking a girls' afternoon to shop. I have budget-conscious ideas for my brother and my parents, and she needs to find something for Clay.

She holds up her phone and I pull up next to her. My attention zeroes in on the numbers on the screen. My friend points a pink-mitten-covered hand at the corner.

"It says I got a thousand new followers overnight."

"Hell, yeah." I tug off my own gloves, cold be damned, and click around her profile.

"It's the video I posted of my work in progress. It's going crazy," she says with wonder.

"People love it." I grin and pass her back the phone. We high-five.

"You're a genius," Nova says as we continue down the block.

I glance up to see the facade of a store that has something I want for my brother. Another patron emerges, and I hold the door for my friend to go first.

"Have you had any new inquiries?" I ask.

"Ten this morning. I can't keep up."

My jaw drops. "Nova. That's insane," I say once we're out of the cold. "If you want, I'd be happy to vet them for you."

"Really? That would be amazing." She does a little skip and a jump that makes me laugh. She types away on her phone. "I'm sending you money now."

The transfer pops up on my cracked screen.

"That's too much," I protest.

"Are you kidding? You got me five times that much new business and saved me a ton of headaches. Plus, without your help, I never would have started selling my art. Or taken the commission for the Kodiaks. Or..."

She's counting items off on her fingers like a shopping list, and I grab her hand out of the air.

"Okay, I get it!"

I love that I was able to help my friend, and the money is a bonus.

"Are you buying something for Miles?" Nova's question interrupts my thinking.

I scrutinize each shelf as I drift down an aisle. "I want to. But I don't want to weird him out."

"How much time have you spent in his bed since the party?"

"Remarkably little," I declare. "On the counter, the dresser, against the wall on the other hand..."

"But this is different because you're exposing yourself," she finishes. "When you get him a present, you're saying, 'This is how I see our relationship and how I value it and what you mean to me.' Which is complicated by the fact that you're living together."

I groan. "Can I just get him a new toaster?"

My thoughts turn to my roommate with benefits. He's done a lot for me, even fully clothed, and I want to show him how much I appreciate him.

We continue browsing until we find what I want for Jay. I search for the wine I want for my mom without luck.

"How hard is it to find a bottle of wine?" I grumble when we get to the register. "I've looked in person, and it was backordered online from the vineyard."

The coffee table at Miles's is strewn with wine flyers, and I've been calling around all week.

"Can you get her something else?" Nova asks.

"This one's her favorite. But I guess it's not happening."

We hit up some thrift stores and are laden down with bags by the time we grab lunch. On our way out, I pause to admire a wall of framed photos of the restaurant over the years. I always thought these displays were kind of kitschy, but something about the black-and-white smiling faces grabs my attention.

A crowd comes in and I finally turn for the door, running smack into another woman.

"Brooke," she says, eyes widening with shock.

"Caroline."

My former sorority sister looks composed as ever, a soft pink wool coat buttoned up to her throat, her cheeks flushed from the cold and her blond hair smoothed into a low ponytail.

Nova's waiting expectantly, so I introduce them.

"Kevin's not here?" I ask, silently willing the answer to be no.

"I'm alone. He's at work," Caroline adds, as if the reason matters. "I've been doing almost all the wedding planning myself."

The reminder that they're engaged elicits a twinge from my stomach, but nothing like when they announced it.

"That must be taxing," I say evenly.

"You have no idea." She cuts a look toward the door, the whites of her eyes shine in the overhead lights.

Under closer inspection, the flush that I attributed to the cold extends across her entire complexion. She's stressed, or maybe sick.

"Are you okay?" I ask Caroline.

Caroline blinks twice. "Perfect. Nice to meet you," she says to Nova.

Trouble in paradise? I wonder.

I should feel vindicated, but most, I feel sad.

"Were you ever friends?" Nova asks as slip out the front doors.

"In the early days at college, I thought we were," I admit. "I don't trust her anymore."

"When you're in a bad moment, it's so easy to forget the good ones."

13

MILES

I'm not the guy to get stressed out. Even in playoffs last year, I wasn't on edge because Clay and Jay had it under control.

Now, I'm our number one option on the court.

That plus the potential endorsement deal are making me sweat.

The midseason tournament is heating up. We're playing the semi-finals today and they're at home.

Lately, my morning routine before a game became getting up and hitting the gym for a quick run before making coffee. It used to be coffee for one, but the past couple weeks, it's for two.

I like making Brooke her almond milk latte. If I have time, I'll decorate the top to make her laugh.

When I get out of the shower this morning, Brooke's already fussing with the machine.

"What're you doing, Princess?"

"Making coffee." She throws up her hands. "The espresso machine only responds to you."

"I have fantastic hands," I agree as I come up behind her and grab her hips.

I figured getting Brooke in bed would soothe the raging beast in my chest.

Instead, I'm plagued by thoughts I've never let myself entertain.

Is she thinking about me like I'm thinking about her?

Does her chest get tight when I enter a room?

Does she look forward to the end of the day, find excuses to come back here when she has a dozen invitations to be somewhere else?

"Want me to take over?" I ask. I've been thinking up some new designs to try out.

"No! I'm going to get it right."

I lean my chin on her shoulder and watch, my lips curving. "You've been taking notes."

"I watched a few videos online," she says breezily as she finishes pulling an espresso.

She holds it out to me and I take a sip. "It's good,"

I say. Her eyes narrow as she takes it back and sips, making a face.

"You're being too nice. I'm starting over."

My gaze drifts to a large cardboard box sitting near the front door. "New espresso machine in case this one lets you down?"

Brooke laughs. "More clothes from *Vivaro*. They agreed the collaboration was a win-win. They're going to pay double for my next posts."

"Hell, yeah." If that box contains more lingerie, I'm sending the CEO a gift basket. "And if I get a fashion show later, it's actually win-win-win."

"Play your cards right," she teases as I pull her closer.

My cock hardens against her ass. "I like making coffee with you in the morning."

"You're wet," she protests as my hair drips on the counter in front of her, but her eyes drift closed when my lips brush her throat.

"So are you." My fingers trace around her stomach and lower, slipping between her thighs.

The espresso machine shoots off a load of steam and Brooke jumps, escaping my grasp.

But she finishes pulling the next one and tests it. "Much better."

I lift her and sit her on the counter.

"How are you feeling about the game?" Brooke asks.

"Super chill." She lifts a brow. "Fine, not great. Plus, Grams has a scan schedule for today." I shake my head. "No idea why she thinks she's going to heal as fast as a twenty-year-old, but she does. Maybe if she had daily physio and other support, it'd be a different story."

Brooke's hand traces my arm. "Does she have an online patient portal? Maybe they'll forward you the scans by email. If you can check them remotely, you won't be thinking about them all day."

The idea lifts a weight off my chest. "You're a genius."

"Anytime." She tilts her head, lips curving and her dark eyes soft.

I've never wanted to kiss someone as badly as I want to kiss her right now. It's not even desire—it's gratitude. The kind that runs bone deep.

She's good at dealing with pressures I've never paid that much attention to.

Brooke takes her coffee and sips it, nodding with satisfaction. "Good luck today. Best way to get that shoe deal is to win."

"Oh, that easy, huh?"

"That easy, champ." Her eyelashes bat over the rim of her mug.

She's so fucking cute.

"You coming to the game today?" I ask.

Her smile stills. "You want me to?"

The questions circling my brain whenever I have a moment of quiet are back.

Suddenly, I'm trying to play it cool.

"Yeah," I say honestly. "I do."

Brooke: Sorry about the L. At least it was close. And Waffles still loves you.

Miles: Thanks. He's legally obliged to.

Brooke: Pity cuddle? I have some new lingerie I'd love your opinion on.

Miles: Home in 30.

14

MILES

"Enough with the pity party," Coach calls at the start of practice. "Semi-finals is respectable work considering we're shorthanded and the West got stronger during the off-season.

"However, this was a rehearsal for the post season, not the post season itself. Which means you've got three more months to get it together."

Sometimes, you're in a groove that takes you out of the effort.

Today is not that day.

I'm playing off-ball, which used to be my comfort zone, but when Jay tries to find me with a pass, I catch it but I'm in the wrong place. My shot is weak, bouncing off the rim with a dull twang.

The next time, Damon stretches out an arm and deflects it before it reaches me.

The third attempt, I miss it altogether. The ball goes sailing into the stands.

Fucking hell.

Jay's gaze finds mine and holds it. There's no mistaking the worry there, and the frustration.

Clay comes up to me on a break. "You play better than you ever have for a few games, and you think you've gotten to a new level. Hell, maybe you have. But there's always a come down."

"Meaning?"

"Last few games, you were so busy scoring it didn't matter that you and Ellis weren't connecting."

Or the fact that Brooke and I are hooking up behind my friend's back is starting to mess with my head.

The first few days didn't bother me because I was too amped to think about anything but memorizing the feel of Brooke's curves under my greedy hands. The taste of her everywhere. The way she hisses my name when she comes.

But it's getting harder to hide from Jay that his little sister is living rent free in my head.

And in my bed.

"You heading out?"

I look up from grabbing my bag on the sidelines of the court to see Jay next to me. "I need to stop at the store, then going to Grams's. You?"

"Going to hit the gym. As my agent reminded me, I have a contract year coming up."

It's a reminder for me, too. There's a ton of pressure in this business, always guys wanting your spot, plus suits making plans and moving pieces around like a chess match. While it would be crazy of the Kodiaks not to try and retain Jay, it's impossible to know what's going on behind the scenes and what other teams have in store.

I haven't spent much time off the court lately with Jay, not only because of Brooke. Life has been busy with Grams and extra training. I miss the downtime, the jokes and the camaraderie that seem to be the first thing to evaporate when you're hunting wins.

"Wait for me."

The Kodiak fitness facility is tricked out with everything you could dream of. When we get there, a handful of guys are working out. Clay's in one corner, headphones on. He nods as we enter but doesn't speak.

I adjust the weight on a barbell and settle onto

the bench. I shift it out of the cups and over my face, Jay moving to spot me.

"So, you sick of my sister yet?" he asks.

My elbows buckle. My grip slips, and the bar descends swiftly toward my face.

Jay catches it halfway to my face. "Shit. Bet you're thanking God for me right now."

He grins, and I exhale hard.

"I mean it though. B's kind of a slob," he adds.

He means as a roommate. Which is the last thing I've thought about over the past two weeks.

"Nah. She's great," I wheeze as I press the bar up. "I like having her around."

It's true. Aside from the part where she's dynamite in bed, Brooke is fun and funny. She calls me out if I'm distracted, presses me to talk about what's on my mind.

I catch myself paying attention to how she looks brushing her teeth in the morning, or the smell of her body wash in the bathroom, or the sound of the hangers in her closet as she riffles through for an outfit in the morning.

"She bring anyone around? Like a guy?" Jay asks.

The next rep has me sweating. "Not lately."

Because the first time went so well.

"I'm glad you haven't seen Kevin. My mom still

loves having him support her campaign, and she thinks Brooke's the best way to get that."

"He shows at my place, I'll rip his preppy head from his body."

Jay's brows lift, but after a moment, he laughs.

"You did that once. Can't afford to get into trouble again."

I take a moment to wipe the sweat from my face with a towel. The gym's familiar scent of rubber and metal fills my nostrils, grounding me.

"Kevin was a piece of shit," I say, my voice low and intense. "Cheating on her, and blaming his drug use on her? That's beyond fucked up."

"I'm glad you were there back then." Jay moves to the bench, getting ready for his set. "Why did you go so hard on him?"

"She deserved better." He hears the edge in my voice. He must, because he doesn't respond right away.

"She was vulnerable," Jay says at last. "Hell, I think she still is. She has this idea like if she acts tough enough, it'll be true."

"Seems like she's in a good place. Better than good," I add without knowing why.

"Maybe." He cocks his head at me. "You would

tell me, right? If she was going through something and you picked up on it."

Guilt burns at my stomach. "Course I would."

But as Jay starts his set and I spot him, the weight of the unspoken truth rests on my chest.

It's heavier than any barbell.

"Special delivery." I knock on the door, shifting the wrapped crate with a bow under one arm. "Hey, Grams."

"Miles, honey."

"Look who I brought." I pull Waffles out of a massive designer tote, and my grandmother beams.

"It was Brooke's idea. And her bag," I admit, turning it so Grams can see the air holes Brooke cut in one side.

"I watched your game the other night. I'm sorry you lost to LA." She pets him while we chat. "You shouldn't have been called for a foul in the fourth. It was a flop."

"Thanks, Grams." Her loyalty warms my heart. I'm not here for her praise, but I'll take it before we get to the topic I came here to broach. "Listen, I want to talk about finding you another place."

Her lined lips press together. "I don't need a new place."

"I'm not trying to change anything you don't want to change. But it worries me when I'm on the road, thinking you might get hurt or need something and I'm not here. I have a couple options." I reach into my back pocket for the flyers I tucked there and hold them out.

She waves them away. "Miles, you can't always be here for me. That's the way life goes."

My gut contracts, a wrongness rising up. "But—"

"I mean it." Her voice has an edge to it.

I drop the topic and we play Monopoly for a bit, but I'm still frustrated over how to move her.

My phone buzzes with a text, and I glance at it quickly. Brooke. Saying she's ordering dinner and she'll get some for me.

I can't help the way my heart kicks.

"That her?"

Grams's eager voice has me looking up.

"Oh. Yeah, it's Brooke." I text a quick thanks and tuck the phone away. "She wanted to make sure Operation Hidden Waffles was a success."

"She destroyed that bag to bring him in here? It must have cost over a hundred dollars."

"Yeah." My lips twitch. I don't have the heart to tell her it was probably way more.

"Things must be going well."

"It's complicated." The response comes immediately, but it feels insufficient for the growing need behind my ribs.

When it's her and me with nothing but sweat and skin, we're golden. She's fun and open and honest.

She doesn't trust relationships, and she has good reasons not to. It's possible I'm the only one wondering if this could be more.

"Then show her. When I was young, if a man liked a woman, he'd make it crystal clear. Unless you don't think she feels the same way?" Grams lifts the empty purse Waffles was in onto her lap, wiggling a finger through the inch-wide holes cut in the sides for ventilation.

I grin and shake my head. "Point taken."

We play a little longer, and she feeds Waffles his body weight in treats. She's still crooning to him when I head into her bedroom under the guise of using the bathroom to wash my hands.

After doing that, I pull the pamphlets from my pocket and tuck them next to her bed under a book.

15

BROOKE

*I*t's not unusual for Denver to get hit with snow weeks or even months before the holidays. Somehow, it came with a vengeance the week before Christmas.

I'm glad the team isn't traveling for their game tomorrow. Even the short drive to our parents' house in Washington Park stretched to nearly an hour.

Jay picked me up this afternoon, his SUV tires protesting on more than one uncleared road in a way that was borderline treacherous.

But the view outside the window is beautiful.

The warm aroma of Mom's famous honey-glazed ham lingers in the air as we finish dinner. Dad pushes his plate away with a contented sigh, while

Jay helps himself to one last scoop of mashed potatoes.

"That was delicious," Dad says, patting his stomach.

Mom starts gathering plates, and I stand to help her. As we stack dishes in the kitchen, I can hear Dad and Jay still chatting at the table.

"How about some after-dinner drinks?" Mom suggests, pulling glasses from the cabinet.

I nod, grabbing the bottle of whiskey Dad likes. "I'll pour."

Back in the dining room, I set glasses in front of Dad and Jay. Mom follows with her signature eggnog for herself and me.

As we settle back into our seats, Mom turns to Jay. "How's the season going? I've been following the games, but it seems like it's been a tough stretch."

Jay sighs, swirling the whiskey in his glass. "We're shorthanded, and some of the Western teams got a lot stronger during the off-season."

"You're doing an amazing job leading the team," Dad chimes in, his voice full of pride. "The way you've been rallying the guys, keeping morale up—that's what real leadership looks like."

Mom nods in agreement, her hand resting on

Jay's arm. "We're proud of you, Jayden. I know it's tough, but you're handling it beautifully."

I sip my eggnog, trying to quiet the emotions swirling inside me.

Jay catches my eye and gives me a smile.

He knows. He's always known how different Mom's expectations are for us.

We have so many shared adventures and memories. My brother might be two years older, but he always respected my opinion, always let me be my own person.

Except he doesn't know the most important things in your life, a voice reminds me.

I've kept from him that Mom cut me off, and she hasn't volunteered it either. Part of me wishes I'd told him, if only so that I don't feel like I'm hiding more than one important development from him.

But so what if I'm sleeping with his teammate? It's not like he has a say in who I date.

Not that Miles and I are dating, but the moments outside of bed are starting to stick with me. The long looks across a room. His endless supply of jokes. The way he whistles as he navigates the kitchen in a towel while making me coffee in the morning. Catching him talking to Waffles as if the Frenchie is a friend and not a foot-high bundle of fluff and attitude.

"So, Brooke," Mom says, turning her attention to me. "How's work going?"

I set my glass down, steeling myself. "I helped Nova land a couple of new jobs."

"Really?" She arches an eyebrow, skepticism evident in her voice.

"Yes. Gallery inquiries. Three commissions with deposits." I try to keep my voice even, fighting the urge to be defensive.

Before Mom can continue, the doorbell rings. We all look at each other, confused.

"You aren't expecting anyone?" Dad asks Mom.

Since no one else is moving, I get up. "I'll get it," I say, grateful for the interruption.

I open the door, and a gust of snow blows in. A little yip of happiness comes from my feet, and I look down to see Waffles, adorned in reindeer antlers, staring up at me.

And then I see Miles, snowflakes dusting his hair and shoulders.

"Hey." I'm breathless, and it's not from the cold air. "What are you doing here?"

"I didn't want to interrupt. Just wanted to bring some holiday cheer." He holds up the bottle of the wine I've been trying to order for my mom.

I can't believe it. "You're unreal." My heart swells with gratitude.

Our hands meet on the bottle, and a zing of electricity passes between us. He grins, and Waffles yips again, pawing at my leg.

"Who is it?" Jay calls from behind me.

"Miles."

Jay appears in the hallway, his face lighting up when he sees Waffles. "Hey, buddy!" He crouches down, and Waffles bounds over, tail wagging furiously.

Mom and Dad join us in the entryway, Mom's eyes widening slightly at the unexpected guests.

"Hey, it's been a long time, Mr. and Mrs. Ellis. Good to see you."

"Miles," my mother says, polite but reserved. "Hello again."

Dad, however, breaks into a warm grin. "Come on in, it's freezing out there."

As Miles steps inside, shaking snow from his boots, Waffles zips around our feet, investigating every corner of the unfamiliar space.

"Oh my," Mom says, eyeing the dog warily. "He's... energetic."

"Waffles is a sweetheart," I assure her, scooping him up. "Here, Mom, want to hold him?"

Mom hesitates, but as I place Waffles in her arms, his little face tilted up adoringly, I see her expression soften. "I suppose he is rather cute," she admits, scratching behind his ears.

Meanwhile, Miles passes over the wine to my dad.

"That's very thoughtful of you," Dad says approvingly.

As we all move back to the living room, Waffles now contentedly curled in Mom's lap, I catch Miles' eye. *"Thank you,"* I mouth. He winks at me, and I feel a flutter in my chest.

"So, Miles," Mom begins, "How did you and Brooke meet?"

"Through Jay," Miles says, glancing at me. "We've known each other for a few years now."

"I see," Mom says, her tone bordering on dismissive. "Well, I do wish you'd known her before she decided to be an internet sales person."

The warmth in my chest fades. "Is this about the *Vivaro* posts?" I cut a look at my brother.

He lifts both palms, but Mom's already going on.

"Brooke, I appreciate that you're less available to help with my campaign this year, but when my team turned up these images, it's not only your brand that's affected."

I open my mouth to respond that I'm not modeling thongs with her campaign slogan on them, but Miles beats me to it.

"With all due respect, Mrs. Ellis," he says, a charming smile softening the firmness in his voice, "Brooke's obviously built an image that people look up to. Hell, my grandmother saw the campaign and wanted to know where she could get leggings like that." My chest tightens. "I can only imagine the hardest thing for her must be deciding what to do, because she's talented, resourceful, and creative. There's only one thing I was ever good at, so it wasn't much of a question."

I stare at him, a rush of gratitude washing over me. It's been so long since someone stood up for me like this, especially to my mother.

Mom looks taken aback.

The tension in the room is palpable, and I'm torn between the urge to smooth things over and the desire to let Miles's words stand.

Finally, Mom asks. "Does your grandmother wear a lot of sports bras?"

Miles laughs first. I join in, cutting a look at Jay, who's also relieved.

"Not lately. She's a pretty good dancer but she's on the injury list right now."

The rest of the conversion is more relaxed and I catch myself enjoying the evening.

"Thanks for the drink," Miles says nearly an hour later. "I should get home. Waffles will be thinking Santa abandoned him."

"The roads are terrible." I'm already up out of my chair before I can think better of it. "You should stay."

Every eye lands on me.

Miles's mouth hangs open. For once, I've caught him off guard.

"I couldn't. You guys are doing family stuff. The Range Rover will be fine."

"Nonsense," Mom cuts in smoothly.

Maybe it's the holiday spirit, or maybe it simply wouldn't look good to have a Kodiaks player in a car accident on the way back from her house on Christmas Eve.

"It'll be great," Jay says, grinning as he rises to clap Miles on the back. "You can borrow pajamas."

16

MILES

*I*t's late when I crack the door and look out into the hallway.

"Stay," I whisper to Waffles, who doesn't lift his head from his spot curled up on the floor.

I take a deep breath, steeling myself, and head down the hall. Everyone else seems to be in bed, the house quiet.

I stand in front of Brooke's room and knock gently on her door.

It's half a dozen heartbeats before the door cracks. Her face appears on the other side, her makeup from earlier scrubbed off and her hair pulled back.

"Everything okay?" she whispers.

"Can I borrow your phone charger? Want to make sure I don't miss my alarm for the morning."

"Oh. Sure thing."

She glances toward the nightstand and I spot the charger there.

I push the door open. She's wearing pajamas too, only hers are silky blue shorts and a button-up top that skims her breasts.

She stifles a laugh at my appearance.

"What?" I protest as I glance down at the borrowed pajamas that are comically short on me.

"You're definitely taller than Jay."

"Six-four."

"And a half."

I grin.

"Is Waffles okay?"

"Yeah. He's out cold in the guest room. Thanks for the hospitality." I try to keep my tone light, even as my pulse quickens. I'm hyper-aware of how close we are, how easy it would be to reach out and touch her.

"I should thank you. You gave me a place to stay all month."

"Why didn't you move in here?" I ask, even though I'm selfishly glad she didn't.

She cringes. "That would mean living under my

mom's expectations, her rules. I wanted to call my own shots and you gave me that."

She takes a step backward, and I follow.

"And thank you for having my back."

The look in her eyes is a confusing mix of emotions. I want nothing more than to pull her close, to show her how I feel. But I'm acutely aware of where we are, of her family sleeping nearby, of her brother down the hall.

"It's a damned privilege to have your back. Not only because it looks every bit as good as your front."

Before I can talk myself out of it, I capture her hand and tug her toward me. The house is silent except for the heater running, dark except for the soft glow of holiday lights through the curtains. I'm lost in her eyes, so beautiful and earnest.

I kiss her.

She inhales in surprise, but her hands skim up my abs to my pecs.

I groan, desire warring with caution. "Princess, we can't do this here."

"You started it," she breathes.

"Fuck. I know."

I can't resist her.

I pull the door closed behind me.

Then I'm kissing her again, my hands diving into

her hair as I tip her face up to mine. She tastes like mint and something that's only Brooke.

"I don't know if I can handle you in my brother's pajamas," she whispers.

"I'll take them off," I murmur back as I kick them down my legs with a grin. "Please handle me."

Her laugh against my mouth is the best fucking feeling in the world.

We stumble across the carpet, and I unbutton her top and push it off her shoulders. The shorts are next, falling in a heap at her feet with a tug from my fingers.

I lift her and wrap her legs around my hips to carry her the rest of the way to the bed.

"Where are you going?" she demands as I set her down and take a step back.

"Want to see you." I search out every inch of her in the darkness. The bright holiday lights outside the window lend a warm glow to her curves.

"You've seen me before." She props herself up on her elbows, her lips parted in a way that makes my dick twitch.

"Yeah, but you're different today." Her head tilts with curiosity. I tell my libido to calm down for a hot second so I can explain. "Seeing you here with your family, I get it. The pressure and the expectations you deal with every day. What you've been raised around. It's a lot."

"Ah, so you can see the stress?" she murmurs with a smile. She's not offended, another thing I love about her. "I think there's a serum for that."

"Nah." I shake my head slowly. "I've never seen you look as beautiful as you do right now."

She reaches for me, and I let her.

As we come together, I'm aware of the intensity of my feelings for her. It's not just physical. I want to protect her, support her, make her laugh. I want to be the one she turns to when she needs strength.

Jay's my friend and teammate, but I saw tonight how important their relationship is, too. The last thing I want is to complicate things or come between them.

So I show her with actions what I'm not ready to say with words.

Afterward, as we lay tangled together, I plug my phone in and set her alarm for 5 a.m. It's risky, staying here, but I can't bear the thought of leaving yet.

"Don't even think of moving before I wake up," I murmur against her ear, tightening my arms around her.

17

MILES

*S*he's in bed next to me when I wake up. Her body is warm, her face tucked into her pillow and her lips parted.

I've never wanted to hit the snooze button so much in my life.

"The hell is that?" Brooke mumbles as I switch off the alarm. "Did I leave my door open..."

Her eyes crack open, and my heart cracks with them.

"Morning," I whisper, aware we have to be quiet.

"Hey."

Her nose points up with a slight curve, and her full lips are parted. Her thick lashes fan across her cheeks.

I lower my mouth to hers, brushing once and then again because I can't resist.

"Merry Christmas, Princess."

"You too."

Her slow smile lights me up.

That's when it hits me.

Brooke Ellis is not a hookup. She's never been a hookup.

Not from the moment as a rookie that I agreed to watch out for her as a favor to her brother.

Not when my fist slammed into another man's face because of what he did to her.

Not once in the years of teasing jokes and half flirting and buried longing since.

The realization is a living thing in my chest.

I can't go another day thinking I could lose her.

In my bed.

In my home.

In my heart.

I glance toward the door. "I should get back to the guest room."

"My mom will be up soon but Jay sleeps like the dead."

"I know. One time when we had adjoining rooms on the road, Rookie and I broke in. We gave him an entire neck tattoo with henna before he woke up."

She laughs silently, her eyes crinkling at the corners.

I pull on the borrowed pajamas as she slides out of bed.

A sound down the hall makes us both glance toward the door. Brooke tiptoes across to crack it.

"Waffles is sleeping in the middle of the hall," she murmurs.

"Shit," I curse softly.

"Don't worry. No one else is up." Brooke returns to the window and opens the curtains. The bright morning light dances on her hair.

"Storm's over," I comment as I straighten, adjusting my pajama pants.

She turns back to me.

"Hope so."

Jay: Merry Christmas Kodiak Fam.

Clay: Let's get a win today.

Rookie: Is there any doubt?

Atlas: Saw you drinking last night so I'd say so.

Rookie: Psssh. It was soda.

Miles: I'm expecting to see a solid cheering section.

Clay: Nova'll be there, and Mari.

Nova: I have the best feeling about this, you guys!

Rookie: Brooke going?

Miles: Yeah.

I'm still hoping me responding to Rookie's question wasn't weird while I make us both coffees.

After having breakfast at her parents' place, we drove back to my place in the Range Rover.

Now, she emerges from her room wearing a jersey.

Every thought in my brain evaporates.

172

"Princess, you look..." I trail off as she turns and I realize it's not my jersey.

It's her brother's.

Of course it is.

She's not going to wear my jersey to a game in front of everyone.

Even if it's suddenly the only thing I want.

"I, uh, have something for you," I say.

"You already got me wine."

"That was for your mom. This is something else."

I get the package. "It's a phone. I didn't know what color you wanted, so I got you three."

"Three?!"

"You can take the other ones back. Or keep them all."

"Thank you. I have something for you too." She grins and bounces off to her room, then returns with a wrapped package.

"Shit, it's so beautiful I feel like a prick wrecking this."

"It's even prettier on the inside."

I scan her with my eyes. "So're you."

"Shut up." Her smile lights me up.

"Nah, I know you're trying to be a brat, but it's too little too late. You can't convince me otherwise with that mouth. Worst that'll happen is I'll have to punish you for it later."

I unwrap the package and my hands still as I see what's in it.

It's a picture frame, or rather a series of them. One of the photos is of me and a few guys from the team before we won. Another is me and my grandma and Waffles back when I was a rookie. Plus one of my parents, smiling on vacation with me as a kid. Of course, I'm still dressed in a hat and basketball shoes even at age ten.

"I found them in your closet," Brooke explains. "I was planning to put them up in the living room, but I wanted to check first."

It feels like a long time since my parents were that happy, since we had anything that looked like a family unit. After they split, I focused on having a big group of more casual friends.

"You just looked like you were having the best time in all of these," she fills in quickly. "No matter what happened before or after, I thought you might want to remember some of the moments that brought you so much joy."

She's right. Looking at these pictures doesn't hurt like it used to.

Brooke shifts on her feet. "But if it's a bad idea..."

"No." I shift the photos into one hand and pull her against my side with the other. "It's a great idea."

BROOKE

Miles: I want to take you on a date

Brooke: A date? I'm at your game - which looking at the clock you should probably get off your phone to play. That must count.

Miles: No way. You, me and 20,000 people is about 20,000 people more than I have in mind.

I meet Nova and the rest of the Kodiaks Fam in the box at the arena.

Mari's here with Harlan, plus Chloe and some other girlfriends and family. There are extra nods to the holiday before the start of the game, including T-shirts made to look like ugly sweaters.

My parents came, plus Sierra and her dad who, one game day a year, stays closed until after the game.

"So much for a relaxing holiday morning," Chloe says, waving her iPad.

"Come on, you love it," Mari interjects.

"Mimosa?" a server asks.

"What the hell." Chloe tucks her tablet under an arm and takes one, toasting with Mari.

The servers pour more mimosas and I take one as I follow Nova to seats at the front of the box.

"Did you guys have a nice time waking up for your first Christmas in your new house?"

"It was better than I imagined." She smiles with a sigh. "It would have been fun to have my fave roommate there though. Did you stay at your parents'?"

"More than just me." I fill Nova in on how Miles wound up staying over last night, skipping the part where he came to my room and we had sex.

Unexpected, hot sex with a surprisingly sweet side.

Forget eggnog. It turns out hooking up in secret with the most popular player in the league in the bed you grew up in is a lip-bitingly decadent holiday treat.

The things he said to me, the way he touched me, felt as if I was the center of his damned universe.

I shouldn't want that from someone. I know from experience that talk is cheap but actually having another person's back is hard.

They announce the starters one at a time, starting with Rookie. Miles is third, jogging out with a sexy smirk and shoulder-bumping Rookie.

It's a turn-on simply watching this man exist.

My brother follows his teammate, offering a wave to the crowd, then an extra one to the box.

"Did you see how Miles jumped on that text this morning?"

I pull out my new phone and open the group chat, studying it. "It's innocent enough. We're roommates."

When I look up, Miles is watching us in the box, his grin heart-stoppingly sexy.

"Right. Roommates." Sierra appears at my other shoulder.

"Nice phone by the way," Nova chimes back in. "When did you find time to have that delivered?"

I angle my chin. "My roommate got it for me. In three colors," I add under my breath.

She hears me, clapping her hands. "Oh, he's got it bad."

The texts he sent me after he went to get ready come back to my mind.

A date with Miles.

After last night, maybe I shouldn't be shocked.

So why does this feel like uncharted territory?

I look between them. "You know you guys are like the angel and the devil on my shoulder, right? Only right now, you're both the devil."

Sierra snorts, shaking her head before leaving to get a drink.

"You're falling for him."

Nova's words, uttered quietly enough we're not overheard, make me snap back.

"No. Not even." I try to laugh, but there's a hint of panic in my throat. "He's beautiful. And thoughtful. And makes the best coffee I've ever tasted. But that's not the same thing."

"Listen. You might be the expert when it comes to branding and how things look. But I see people as they are, and that man is *in it* with you."

My heart stops as I watch him.

What would it look like to actually have a relationship? One not based on us being roommates, or the illicit thrill of sneaking around behind my brother's back?

How long before he expects me to do and be things that I don't want?

The shadow of Kevin is still there, even after all these years.

"You think I should go for it." I bite my lip, my eyes never moving from the court.

"I think you deserve to be happy, and I haven't seen you smile as much as you do when you're around Miles Garrett."

18

BROOKE

Growing up, our holidays were filled with social commitments and photo sessions and expectations.

This year's was surprisingly fun by comparison.

The Kodiaks won their game to the deafening roar of a home crowd dressed in purple and gold with matching Santa hats.

My mom even asked if I would help her with messaging for her campaign in the new year, a task she usually leaves to her highly trained staff.

There's a box of *Vivaro* product that's still sitting unopened in my room because I've been busy monitoring Nova's accounts and helping her progress conversations with a couple of galleries wanting to host shows.

My friend wants to give everyone a chance, but I'm ruthless with weeding out curators and owners with a less than stellar reputation, or ones who are interested in Nova's connections rather than her art itself.

It's addictive, and seeing the joy and delight on my friend's face when I present them to her makes it even better.

The Kodiaks have a two-game road trip and will return on New Year's Eve, but for today, they're at home.

That means Miles is home and this tenuous more-than-roommates, less-than-dating thing we have is front and center in my mind.

"Where are we going?" I ask as I emerge from my bathroom.

"Surprise." Miles looks me up and down, his eyes glinting.

He's wearing jeans and a designer sweater the same color as his eyes. He fills the entire doorway of his room in a way that makes me think they should make bigger entrances for basketball players.

The way I'm sore from last night... they definitely should.

His fingers thread through mine as we take the elevator down to the parking garage.

Watching him burn up the court yesterday was the best foreplay. I was ready to climb him like a tree after the game, but we both had family stuff to do.

"I guess this is our first real date," I say as I shift into the passenger side of the Range Rover, sliding on my Prada sunglasses.

Miles has the gall to look offended over the lapel of his wool coat. "I took you out for pancakes at Denny's back in college."

"That was different. You were watching out for me," I say as he navigates toward the exit of the lot.

When he pauses for traffic before turning onto the road, he glances toward me. "I might have checked you out once or twice."

"Stop it." I pull my glasses down my nose and stare at him over them.

His grin, as blinding as the sun outside, makes my heart do a little flip.

As we drive to our mysterious location, I watch the buildings fly past.

If I want to leave by the start of January, which was the plan all along, I need to nail down a new apartment. I also haven't mentioned it to my current roommate.

Miles's phone rings, and he glances at the number. "My agent," he says. "I can call him back."

"No. It could be important."

He hits accept. "What's up."

"Just heard something on the shoe deal. You're not going to like it."

Miles's hand tightens on the steering wheel. "Tell me."

"It shouldn't come as a surprise, but they're courting two other players. Guys that have exceeded expectations going into the break, apparently."

"Anyone I know?"

"They wouldn't confirm, but I got word that one is Hawkins, out of Boston."

My nose wrinkles. Jay doesn't make enemies easily, but the guy is one of my brother's least favorite players.

"So the fact that we didn't win the midseason tournament means my stock is falling," Miles reads.

"That's what I'm trying to find out. Sit tight. Wouldn't hurt you to keep putting up twenty-five a night with a wholesome smile."

"That easy, huh?"

"That easy."

His agent clicks off and Miles frowns as he navigates.

I reach over to lay a hand over his. "You're not

out yet. They're probably just doing their homework."

I vow to take his mind off it, even before he pulls up in front of a faded façade.

I let out a laugh. "You know how to wow a girl."

"For the woman who has everything. Eight ninety-nine all-day breakfast."

We get out, and he holds the door for me to go inside the Denny's. The hostess finds us a booth with a little privacy. There's still a chance of us being seen, and he shifts in on the same side as me.

"Two coffees, please," he orders.

The waiter's expression lingers a little on Miles. Then he looks at me and mouths, "Lucky."

I smile and wink.

"How's the phone working?" he asks.

"I'm sticking with the bright blue one. If you tell me how to return the others, I'll do it this week."

Miles shakes his head. "No way."

"What do you mean? You didn't keep the receipts?"

He shrugs, sheepish. "You can't take them back. The gold one reminds me of your eyes. And the red one goes with those sparkly shoes you wore to the Halloween party."

My chest expands until it feels like I've

swallowed a helium balloon. "Fine. Well, the blue one is lucky. Elise reached out to wish me happy holidays on my social story I put up from the box."

"You think you've still got a shot?"

"Or she was just being polite and felt bad about how things ended." I shrug.

"I can't help feeling a little responsible. Me groping you in the hot tub lost you the gig."

I slant him a look. "In a weird way, I'm glad it didn't work out. Helping Nova with her business has been more fun than worrying about my own brand. It takes the pressure off her, and I get to put my skills to use and spend time with the people I care about."

Our coffees arrive and we put in the rest of our order.

My hands wrap around the mug. I take a sip, aware of Miles watching.

"Does it beat mine?" he asks, lips curving.

I frown, pretending to debate. He nudges me under the table with his foot.

"Jury's still out," I decide.

He groans.

Except it doesn't beat his. Not even close.

There are no layers to the flavor. There's no heart drawn on it with steamed milk, like the most recent one he made me.

Which wouldn't be disturbing except that I'm starting to wonder if it's not only about the coffee.

What if Miles Garrett beats everyone else where I'm concerned?

At *everything*?

I can't resist asking, "So what is this? Some do-over of the last time you took me for breakfast?"

"I wanted to do it again, now that I get to look at you and touch you. Now that I get to give a shit."

As much as his words make my heart skip, there's a bigger question I've been debating asking. "Why *did* you give a shit?"

Miles turns it over. "You've always had this inner strength I admired. I wanted to protect you. When Jay said that he told you the truth about Kevin... he didn't tell you all of it, because he didn't know. The truth is I cared way too fucking much about you. I hated that he put you at risk and made you hurt. I wanted to hurt him twice as bad."

"You knew Kevin was cheating on me," I blurt.

Miles holds my gaze for a long time before he nods.

"The drug stuff on top of that, the fact that he used you, took things to another level."

I shake my head. "I must have seemed so naive."

"No. He was just unworthy."

Miles says it as if it's obvious, but my chest contracts.

No one's ever spoken that way before, about Kevin or me.

But now that we've started, more questions tumble to the front of my mind.

One drowns out the others.

"You were on a rookie contract." I lower my voice, aware of the patrons around us. "What you did to Kevin could've gotten you kicked out of the league and ended your career. I'm surprised he didn't press charges."

Miles shifts back in his seat. "Yeah, well. It sure wasn't out of the goodness of his heart. I got pictures of him in some compromising situations."

"What you're saying is..."

Miles takes a long sip of coffee. "Mutually assured destruction."

There's nothing but conviction in his tone.

It's a reminder that Miles Garrett, most popular guy in the league, seems to have an edge when it comes to me.

Maybe I should be concerned by it, but I've seen enough people dig in for their own interests over the years. Having someone go hard to defend mine makes me want to let him in.

But it's one thing on let a person in, and another to lean on them.

"I appreciate how you've been there for me. Then, and now. And I promised both of us I'd only impose on you for a few weeks."

His brows pull together. "Brooke—"

"Let me finish. I said I'd be out by the New Year. And between my brand work and Nova, I actually have a positive bank account balance. It feels good. But." I take a breath. "I don't want to be reckless and wind up without savings in another month. So to be sensible, it might be best if I stayed another couple of weeks if you're okay with that."

"No."

Dismay hits me. "No?"

"No, I don't want you moving out in two weeks."

His meaning sinks in.

"Miles. I'm not saying we have to end whatever this is. But you must miss having your own space."

"I don't. And if you try to say you don't like me, or that I'm a bad roommate, there's an empty jumbo box of condoms that prove otherwise."

He threads his fingers through mine, tracing my palm with his thumb. "What do you say, Princess? Stick around a minute. Play this out with me. I don't know where it'll go, but I'm dying to find out."

My throat is tight. I always have a response, whether it's right or wrong, but now, I'm speechless.

"I guess I'm not in a hurry." The words are casual but they feel anything but.

His handsome face splits into a grin. "There's one more thing. As much as I love sneaking around with you, I don't want to keep hiding this. Not from the team."

"And by the team you mean my brother," I finish.

Miles exhales hard. "Pretty much."

"You think he'll hate it?"

"I don't know."

I wrestle with the idea. The Kodiaks need this road trip.

Miles needs this road trip, to keep his chances of this deal alive.

"Let's keep it under wraps until New Year's," I suggest. "We'll tell him when you get back."

19

MILES

*M*iami is a bitch.

They're only the start of a long ass stretch against Eastern teams that features New York and our nemesis—at least as far as Jay's concerned—Boston.

Hawkins has been watching our games and going off on his own social. Every time he does, I hear about it from Jay at practice.

Here's hoping the shoe sponsor is going to decide he doesn't fit with their "wholesome" brand before I have to score another basket.

Either way, the Kodiaks have a secret weapon.

Atlas is back.

Okay, so he was only approved to play five minutes by the team's trainers. After the first two months of the season without a true center, we'll take what we can get.

Miami chirps less than Boston, in the media and on the court, but they're solid and pissed after the last time we beat them. We need to string together new momentum after our loss in the midseason tournament right before the holidays.

It's a gritty game. They're physical from the tip off.

Jay's a step slow.

"Come on, man. You've got this," I say to him after they strip the ball from Jay's hands in an uncharacteristic steal going the other way.

He doesn't respond, already digging in on defense.

"Ellis. Get it together," Clay grunts at him a few plays later.

Jay shakes his head and grumbles words I can't hear because of the hollering Miami fans.

At halftime, we start to turn it around.

Atlas's appearance off the bench gives us a much-needed boost. Coach sat Jay, who claimed he wasn't feeling right, for a couple of extra shifts, and the rest of the starters pull it together. My shooting line doesn't suck either.

We get it tied by the time the clock runs out.

Overtime.

The final five minutes feels like fifty.

We lose 110-106.

The vibe in the locker room ranges from exhausted to frustrated to despairing.

Jay seems ready to punch something.

It's one thing to win when you deserve it, but winning pro basketball games is a group effort.

Tonight, we didn't have the group to win.

Brooke: Sorry about the L.

The text comes in after I've stripped off my jersey and am getting ready to head for the shower.

Miles: Thanks Princess. Do I get a pic to console me?

"Hey man, we going out after media?" Rookie's voice is distant.

I'm ready to go back to my room and call Brooke.

Never used to like having someone sending me

messages on the regular, but with her, I'm living for every damned notification.

At the same time, keeping our relationship from my team weighs heavier than ever.

She suggested waiting until we got back to break the news.

But she's also not the one who has to look her brother in the eye for hours a day.

"Miles?" Rookie appears from nowhere at my shoulder.

I slam the phone facedown on the bench. "What?"

"Whoa. You been testing new coffee recipes? Step away from the espresso machine, my friend." Rookie goes back to his locker, chuckling.

He's not wrong that I'm on edge.

Every second we're on the court together, anytime Jay shouts for me, the lie is burning in my chest, thudding against my ribs.

I flip the phone. There's an image of Waffles in a tiny purple jersey.

The laugh rumbles out of me without warning.

Brooke: It even has your number on the back.

Miles: Someone else I'd rather see wearing it.

Brooke: Play your cards right and you might.

Miles: Tonight? After media I'm all yours.

Brooke: You're cute when you talk to reporters. I might have to start without you.

Miles: I'm counting on it.

Brooke: Got a codeword just for me?

Miles: Houseplant

Brooke: LOL WHAT?

Miles: Yup. I say houseplant and I want you coming on the biggest toy you have.

"We're going out," Atlas decides.

I drag my attention away from my phone. "I'm going to pass." I stretch an arm across my chest. My lats are still complaining from lifting yesterday.

"You can't pass." Jay's voice is aggressive. "Even Clay's coming. Right?"

We all turn to look at our all-star, a tight-lipped wall of tattoos.

Clay grunts. "Why not?"

Rookie jumps in. "Hell yes. There's this salsa club my cousin works at, and they can get us a great booth."

"What was that shit about houseplants?" Rookie calls over the music.

"Good to have a green thumb." I nurse a beer at the bar next to him.

It's hard to hold onto a bad mood in this place. There's an epic DJ with Cuban music pumping through the floor. Bartenders are salsa dancing on the other side of the bar, cheered on by patrons.

Sure, I would rather be back in my hotel room, video-calling Brooke, but team bonding is important, especially after a loss. These are the moments that will build us up, get us back on track with three short months until the playoffs.

"We needed that win." A blonde woman leans over, her smile inviting.

"Thanks. I'll admit that doesn't make me feel a lot better." I lift both hands.

She bites her lip. "I could make you feel better."

"As generous as that offer is, I'm going to pass."

"You're very hands-off," Jay observes when the woman turns back to her friends. "That's at least a dozen times you've gotten hit on tonight."

"Trying to keep my focus where it needs to be." I take a drink of my soda. "Surprised you came out. How're you feeling?"

"No complaints."

He says it so fast I'm frowning. "Yeah? Because earlier, you were..." I trail off as he orders a second drink.

Or his third.

"You seemed out of it," I finish.

"Come on. You're not taking any of the blame?"

I shake my head. "Sure, man. I know it's been hard lately on the court. But we're figuring it out. We're friends, and I've got your back."

"Do you? Feels like you don't tell me shit anymore." Jay reaches for his beer, tipping it back.

"When did it start?" he asks when he sets the bottle down, half empty.

The inflection is at odds with the tension in his voice.

"What?" I ask, even though I know.

"You hooking up with my sister. Before or after you moved her in with you?"

It never occurred to me Jay would find out. Maybe it should have, but the longer it went on, the more protected I felt.

If I'd imagined all the ways a confrontation could go down, at a bar on the road after a hard loss would have been my nightmare scenario.

"Before." I pause. "How'd you find out?"

"That's what you want to know?" He laughs, cursing. "No. You don't get to ask me fucking questions right now."

"It's not what you think." I go to reach for his shoulder but he shoves my hand away, knocking it into his beer.

The bottle spins, spilling across the surface. Rookie catches it, glancing over with surprise, but Jay isn't paying any attention.

"No? You don't remember me saying to look out

197

for her? That I didn't want anyone on the team moving in on her?"

Jay's not a physical guy, but he takes things personally. The guy's helped me when I've screwed up before. But the way he's looking at me, the accusation on his face...

I'm realizing what a mistake it was to put off telling him the truth.

"She's had a hard time. You know this more than anyone, yet you're sliding up next to her like a shoulder to cry on."

Guilt flares in my gut, even though I know he's wrong. That's not what happened.

"I'm sorry for not telling you the truth sooner. We were going to."

"Oh, you were."

"We can get past this. For the sake of our friendship. For the team."

His eyes narrow as he considers. "You want to make this right?" I nod. "Then don't."

"Don't what?"

"Don't touch her. Don't look at her. Get her the hell out of your apartment. Find somewhere else to stick your dick."

I lean back against the bar and take a slow breath.

He doesn't know how in this I am, that it isn't some casual thing.

I didn't decide one day I'd replace the revolving door of girls with Brooke. I've known on some level she was who I wanted for longer than I'm willing to admit.

For some reason, I can't bring myself to say the words.

That I'm falling for her.

That the idea of her leaving is laughable.

That what's responsible for me being the player and the man I am lately is Brooke.

"Those are your options, Garrett. You're going to have to decide what's important."

He spits the words before turning on his heel and vanishing, leaving a pit in my stomach and half the Kodiaks team staring after him.

20

BROOKE

*J*ay and I used to fight a lot as kids. My mom didn't like it because I was younger and a girl, but he'd still kick my ass.

I'd come right back at him next time with new moves.

But ever since I got the text from Miles, I've been on edge.

Miles: Jay knows.

I could reach out to try to fix this, but I've done nothing wrong. That's what I tell myself anyway. I'm a grown woman who can date who she wants.

Tonight though, Mom asked if I could come for dinner, so I head over there as the sun is setting.

Over our grilled salmon, Mom asks, "Have you reached out to Caroline lately?"

"I ran into her shopping before Christmas."

"If you kept in better touch, you could be a bridesmaid."

I reach for my water, coughing. She watches in alarm as I chug it.

"Excuse me. I just laughed."

My mother sighs, exchanging a look with my dad.

"How's your campaign going?" I ask.

She takes another bite of dinner, chewing thoughtfully.

"In my most recent speech, I overstated our commitment to funding on a particular program. If we issue a correction, it'll look like we're backing away from what we promised. If we don't, my competition could raise it."

"Which program?"

"After-school programming for children."

I think it over. "You have donors interested in that. Why don't you go to them and tell them what happened? Admit you misspoke, but tell them you'd like to meet that commitment. See if they'll help."

"That's admitting my personal mistake to the

people who fund my campaign. They'll question my competence and whether they invested in the right place."

"Or they'll see that you're human and appreciate your willingness to confide in them."

She shakes her head. "Perhaps I was hasty cutting you off. I could use your help with this campaign."

"I'm keeping busy. I've been working with Nova to schedule new shows and sales. Tomorrow, I'm helping Chloe with the Kodiaks New Years Eve fundraiser. And in between, I'm doing this *Vivaro* collaboration."

While Miles was away, I went through the box of product they sent. There are some items I'm excited about.

"Tell me you didn't commit to more than a post."

"Why not? They've been straightforward to work with and prompt to pay."

One brand partnership isn't enough to sustain me forever, but it will help me to start a savings account, and be a huge stepping stone for future deals.

"They *will* want more," she promises, "and they'll expect you to fall in line. The world expects women who look like us to conform. To be grateful for every opportunity."

"Like you expect me to?"

Mom's eyes sharpen. "I'm trying to prepare you. And protect you."

"I have a roof over my head, and I'm doing fine. Better than fine."

As I head toward the kitchen with a casserole dish, I hear the front door opening.

My dad warmly greets Jay in the background. I continue to the kitchen and set the dish in the sink.

"Pretending to wash dishes, huh? You haven't washed a dish in years."

I glance over my shoulder to see my brother leaning against the doorframe. "I know you're not here to compliment my domestic abilities."

"You and Miles have been sneaking around behind my back."

I turn to face him, folding my arms. "I'm living with him. We were clearly trying to dodge you."

Jay cocks his head. "You both had a hundred opportunities to say something. You didn't."

"It's new!" I throw up my hands. "And as much as you hate to admit it, it wasn't about you. On the court, it might be your job to boss people around, but when the whistle blows? You don't get to say how I spend my time or with whom."

I turn back to the sink and start furiously scrubbing the dish.

"Yeah, because you were such a great judge of character with Kevin."

My hands still, my spine straightening. "Like you've never made a mistake before? I can't believe you're bringing that up."

Jay's voice is contrite. "You're right, that was low. But I'm your brother."

"I didn't want to bother you."

"Because you didn't think I would care?"

He's angry, but more than that, he's hurt. That's the only reason I try to hang onto my last shred of patience.

I slam the clean dish down next to the sink, hard enough the sound echoes. "Because I knew you'd overreact. When Mom cut me off, I needed someone to have my back, and Miles was—"

"When what?!"

Shit.

"When did this happen?"

I grab for a dish towel to dry my hands. "A month ago."

"And Garrett knew about it." He's gone from hurt to incredulous.

My hands fist in the fabric.

Forget patience. My dear brother is digging himself a hole even I can't help him out of.

"You just can't handle the fact that you didn't have a say in it. Newsflash, Jayden: you might be a point guard for eighty-two games a year, but not everyone in the universe waits for your permission to do things. Miles doesn't. I don't." Seething anger rises up. "Chloe damn well didn't."

His eyes widen.

Before I can decide whether to take it back, my mom sticks her head in.

"Miles? You're dating Miles Garrett?" she demands. Her fingers grip the doorframe.

"It's nothing," Jay states.

"It's not nothing." I throw my towel at him, and he catches it, surprised.

I turn on my heel and stalk out.

MILES

Miles: Not going to lie, I was hoping to come home to a prettier face than Waffles.

"Dude, you missed that one." Rookie nods to the flatscreen television.

We're sitting on the couch playing video games at my place when a text comes back. I glance down at the phone at my side.

Brooke: Nova and I are helping Chloe prep for the gala. It's going to be a late night so I might crash here after.

I almost forgot about the team's NYE party tomorrow night.

I hit pause on the game despite Rookie's protests and type back.

Miles: Anything I can do?

Brooke: I'm fine. Thanks though.

. . .

I'm disappointed she's not coming back tonight.

More than that, I'm worried about her. She's acting tough but I want to know what she's not telling me. If she was here, I could coax it out of her.

I want to touch her, to look her in the eyes. As if it will somehow reassure me that I'm right about the stand I took in front of my friend and point guard.

"Jay's not coming, huh?" Rookie asks.

"Probably not."

Jay was supposed to join us, but I'm guessing since he found out about me and Brooke, we're out.

I shift back and drop the phone to my side.

Rookie turns to face me, face tight with worry. "You think tomorrow's going to be more or less weird than the ride home?"

The flight back from Miami on BearForce One was awkward as hell. Jay was at the one end of the plane with Atlas and Clay, me at the other with my headphones on pretending to nap.

"Can't believe you went there with his sister." Rookie's voice has me looking up.

"She's not his sister." I mash the buttons on my controller. "She is," I go on at his expression, "but she's more than that. It was a long time coming."

"So I never had a chance?"

The possibility drifts through my mind, making my lip curl. "Not if you wanted to live."

He turns that over as we go back to the game.

"We were going to tell him after the road trip." I need a damned massage because my shoulders feel like one big-ass knot.

"This going to fuck shit up for the team?" Rookie asks. He's a confident guy, but he's also twenty-one and needs a contract next year.

"I won't let it," I promise.

21

BROOKE

"It's got to be here." Chloe rifles through the back of her sleek white SUV.

"What are we looking for?" The back is piled high with clear bins, but because there must be a dozen or more, it's hard to find one in particular.

"A box of special edition uniforms the guys wore last month. Worn merch always makes the most at the charity auction."

I wrinkle my nose. "I get that fans want original jerseys, sweat and all—but clearly none of them grew up with a basketball player leaving gross dirty clothing everywhere."

When I found out that Chloe was organizing the charity gala, I promised to help. It took my mind off things with Miles and my brother.

The jerseys turn up in two separate bins, and we carry them into the hotel via the back entrance.

Members of the Kodiaks organization, including the players, are distributed amongst tables for dinner. Chloe already had my brother sitting with an avid outdoorsman so they could talk about their love of camping, but I noticed that Rookie and a local CEO had attended the same college, and suggested it made more sense to put Damon, the new recruit who was boasting about his new microbrewing project, with the retired pharmaceutical exec who spends his winters skiing in Colorado and his summers at his vineyard in Sonoma.

The gala is in a massive ballroom. Staff are completing a final review of décor just as caterers are starting to circulate with canapes and VIP guests are arriving.

It might not be the worst idea that the players are split up. I see my brother on the other side of the room in what looks like a tense conversation with a couple of other players.

Not going there.

Next, my gaze lands on another tall, athletic form that's almost directly opposite my brother.

Miles.

There's no mistaking the dark, wavy hair, the

broad shoulders in that perfectly cut tux, or the sound of his laugh amongst the small group of non-Kodiaks he's entertaining.

Unlike my brother, he gets it. This is about the community, not the team.

I'm filled with gratitude, and pride.

As if feeling my attention, he turns. His gaze lands squarely on me.

In an instant, he excuses himself from the conversation he's in. He stalks toward me, leaving the ballroom for the hallway even as I take a step back.

"Princess." His eyes are a thousand feet deep right up until his attention drops to the bin in my arms. "You giving away my clothes so you can take the entire closet?"

"Close. Setting up auction items in the next room."

He nods, and I hand him the bin.

"Nice game the other night," Chloe says.

He blinks when he realizes she's there. "Thanks, Chlo."

"You've been working hard. Except for the media stuff about houseplants. Don't go off script like that tonight."

"No promises," he deadpans. "I've been known to say some crazy shit."

"Yeah, no more houseplants stuff. Keep the gardening private."

I narrowly avoid tripping on the carpet.

Chloe looks at Miles, then me, then shakes her head, sending her shiny black hair sliding over her shoulders.

We walk to the next room, a smaller ballroom setup with auction items. The Kodiaks do a significant amount of charity work, and tonight is one of their major initiatives in support of the Kodiaks Camp for children.

Miles sets the bin where Chloe directs him.

"I have to get to James. The owner's been blowing up my phone for half an hour," she says.

"I'll finish putting these out," I promise.

"Really? You're the best." She squeezes my arm with a grateful smile.

Suddenly Miles and I are alone, or as alone as we can be with tuxedo-clad staff bustling around the beautiful hotel.

His gaze lowers to my outfit. "You look beautiful."

My fingers slip on my task. "Thank you. You look all right yourself." He's in a navy suit that highlights the blue of his eyes.

I set out the jerseys, fussing with them so they're displayed to their best advantage.

"You okay? I was worried when you didn't come home last night."

Home.

Is it crazy that part of me wishes it was? That a temporary landing spot feels more and more like the kind of sanctuary I never realized I wanted?

"Jay came over to my mom's last night."

I spend a little extra time on Miles's jersey, feeling the fabric between my fingers. Someone's going to buy it tonight just to have a piece of him.

Miles shifts between my task and me, forcing me to stop. "If he was an asshole—"

"He had a few thoughts."

Miles's jaw flexes.

I don't need him to stand between me and my brother, but before I can say so, we're interrupted.

"Guys!" Chloe calls from the doorway. "James is getting started."

We follow her into the ballroom, where the team's owner is calling everyone to attention. Dotted around the room are the Kodiaks, management and coaching staff, plus significant others.

"You better get back to your assigned seat or Chloe will have your ass," I whisper to him.

For a moment, I think he's going to say "Fuck it," but he reluctantly heads toward his designated spot.

"Tonight is about the city and the team," James reminds the room. "There are five hundred VIPs out there, so everyone needs to be on their best behavior. The stakes are getting higher at this point in the season. The all-star game is coming up soon, and after that, the playoffs. We need everyone to pull together on this."

Appearances matter.

I focus on that.

I float around, being an extra Chloe and making sure the donors are having a great time. I head over to the auction room, adding color commentary to the items to help get the bids up.

"You need a drink," a familiar female voice says at my back, making me turn.

"I need a few," I respond under my breath.

Nova beams. My friend looks stunning, her blond-and-pink hair pinned up on her head.

I wave over a bartender dressed in a black tux who serves us champagne.

Once we've clinked glasses and taken a sip, Nova say, "Have you talked with Jay since last night?"

I shake my head. I filled her in on everything last night when I stayed at her place.

Her eyes cloud. "What did Miles say?"

"He was in team meetings all day today, so the first time I saw him was here. Maybe we should talk about something else."

"Like my business? I already have more shows lined up for the new year than ever."

Pride for my friend rises up. "You're incredible."

"We make a good team," she corrects.

I excuse myself to go to the bathroom to freshen up, still thinking over her words about making a good team.

The Kodiaks make a good team. Good enough to win a championship.

Unless something does irreparable damage.

I haven't seen Miles and my brother within twenty feet of each other all night. Not that I've been watching for that, exactly, but it's on my radar.

When I re-enter the ballroom, the countdown to midnight is on. The team is together, hollering and raising their glasses. A couple of gazes fall on me, new guys on the team, curious rather than friendly.

Like I'm a story they've heard about rather than a real person.

Discomfort has me vacating the ballroom for the smaller auction room, which still has guests, but far fewer.

And no prying eyes.

In my Kappa days in the aftermath of Kevin's drug issues, I felt that way all the time.

"You ran out of here pretty fast." Miles is behind me.

"Normal need-to-fix-my-lipstick speed." I glance around us. "Figured you'd want to watch the ball drop with the team."

"Don't blame me wanting to be close to the most beautiful woman in the place."

My chest warms.

"What did he say to you?" His brows form a dark slash across his handsome face.

"Nothing I need to repeat." I paste on a smile, aware of everyone around us. "I love him, even when I wish I didn't. But he's always had this way of dismissing things that mattered to me if he didn't understand them, or they didn't fit with what he wanted."

"All right, then I'll tell you what he said to me. He told me to stop. To end things with you."

His words make the breath stick in my throat. "And what did you say?"

"I'm not going to do that. You matter. We matter." Miles captures my wrists loosely in his huge hands. "I can't be sure of everything in my life right now, but I want this."

My heart kicks so hard I think my ribs will bruise.

"Jay'll have to get over it." He strokes my skin with his thumbs. "Because Princess, I don't want to get over you."

The backs of my eyes sting.

We're surrounded by people but he's the only one I see.

This man who's been in my life for way too long, but somehow snuck up on me when I wasn't looking.

"Three! Two! One!"

The crowd choruses, jumping in on the countdown.

I'm lost in Miles's eyes.

When the clock hits zero, I press up on my toes and fist my hands in his white shirt.

He's already kissing me back.

22

BROOKE

"Wait." I hold up a hand by the doors and slip off my shoes.

"You're not walking like that out to the car."

"Watch me."

Before I can protest, Miles scoops me up in his arms. My fingers grip the back of his neck, his hair soft against my fingers.

The automatic doors slide wide as he carries me to the parking lot and doesn't set me down until we're at the Range Rover.

He helps me inside and moments later, we're backing out of the spot.

"Are you drunk?" I ask.

"You think I'd drink alcohol and drive you around?" He shakes his head, perplexed.

"Not really. But I'm trying to think of why else you'd say what you said back there."

"Because I mean it. Because it's true."

My heart kicks.

Miles cares enough to stand up for us against the team.

Sure, Jay's way out of line, but he's their leader and he tried to pull rank.

My roommate, the easygoing joker with the fast smile and the wicked grin, told him where to put it.

"You're not putting me down?" I ask when we get back to the condo and Miles carries me out of the car and steps into the elevator.

"Nope."

I press the button.

The elevator dings and he carries me down the hall. "Gonna need you to swipe us in."

I reach into my bag for the key. The door swings open, and he carries me inside. Waffles yips a couple of times from the corner, then goes back to sleep.

Miles carries me into his room. He doesn't set me down until I'm over the bed.

"That was impressive."

He pushes a hand through his hair. "I work out."

I burst out laughing, and he grins.

But there's been a need bubbling beneath the surface.

We've always had chemistry, but this feels like something else. When things aren't right in the world, he has this magical way of making them right *with him*.

I want his skin on mine, each piece of us lined up. I want to lay my heart on his and say, "See? They sound the same."

I press up on my knees, and he bends down to meet me. When I grab his face and pull him to me for a soft kiss, he's surprised for half a second at most. His athlete instincts kick in and he kisses me back.

Miles's mouth is full of need, but it's the generosity that gets to me.

His hands skim up my thighs with a reverence that steals my breath. The room is impossibly dark, at least until he lights a candle on the nightstand that casts a warm glow over everything.

"We've got time," he murmurs.

And that sets the pace.

Each touch turns slow and languid and sensual.

Miles might not think of himself as a romantic guy, but he is. He notices me, his expression saying he appreciates every damn move I make whether it's right or wrong.

He takes off my dress. The buttons are tiny, but he won't let me help. The stubborn movements turn me on even more, my hands skimming along his biceps as he works.

"Not helping," he murmurs against my neck.

"Sorry," I lie, going to work on the buttons on his shirt.

Minutes later, my dress is tugged gently over my head and dropped on the floor. His suit jacket and shirt too.

It's thousands of dollars of clothes.

Neither of us cares.

His lips trace down my throat to my breast and find my nipple, and he tugs with his teeth. I inhale sharply. My fingers thread in his hair as he sucks me.

The candle on the nightstand flickers, making everything look like a dream. The way his arms band around my hips. The softness of his hair as he angles his head, moving to the other side.

It's like he knows me.

Maybe he does.

I reach for his pants, but he brushes away my hands. His lips skim down the curve of my stomach as he traces a hand up the back of my thigh. I sway toward him.

"I've always liked road trips," he murmurs. "Get to see a new city. Catch up with friends."

He strips off my tights and panties, then tugs one of my knees wider.

I grab his shoulder for balance. His lips brush the inside of my thigh, whisper soft.

"Hell, I even sleep great in hotel rooms."

He strokes lightly between my thighs. It's the barest stroke, but my breathing hitches.

"But lately, I can't sleep worth shit. Every second I'm wishing I was right here..."

Miles's fingers stroke the length of my pussy, dipping in a few inches.

"...with you..."

He grabs my ass and pulls me toward his face.

"Doing this."

The sensations wash over me in a wave of pleasure.

His tongue stroking my clit.

His fingers pressing inside me.

He goes to work as if it's his greatest joy and every sound I make, every shiver of my body, is the only response he needs.

The temptation is too strong, the desire too close. I'm riding his fingers and grinding against his face. His fingers dig into my ass.

"Say my name." He groans it. "Say my name when you come on my face, Princess."

When my body goes tight, that sweet pleasure bordering on pain then exploding into weightlessness, there's nothing on the tip of my tongue except his name.

No words, no thoughts, no desires that aren't him.

My body trembles, and he fucks me through it until I'm gasping and begging him to stop. Then he lays me back, lying on one side to look down at me. He traces my shoulder with a finger. The candlelight warms us both.

"That was fucking spectacular."

"Isn't that my line?" I tease.

"I was talking about you." His lips brush mine. "I'm glad you used the jacuzzi when I was on the road."

"I might need to again."

"If you're ready for round two—"

"I meant for my sore feet." I laugh.

His hands slide down to my feet and he caresses them, pressing his thumb into my arch. My head twists, my cheek rubbing the pillow. I could die happy.

"Damn it, is there anything you're not good at?" I manage.

"Staying away from you." His smile is oddly shy.

I twist out of his grip, rearing up onto my knees so we're chest to chest. I grab his face with both hands. "Don't ever."

The words takes everything inside me, because I'm admitting I want him, I need him.

This time, his lips are hungry. He kisses me as though he's desperate, and I kiss him back as if he's the answer to a question I've been too afraid to ask.

He rises and strips off his pants and shorts before returning to me. His length is impossibly thick and hard. I circle him with my fingers anyway.

I lower my lips to him, kissing his tip until he growls. "Come on now. I'm too amped for that."

I take him in, swirling my tongue around him. His string of curses makes me grin.

"Take it like a man, Garrett." I look up at him from under my eyelashes.

He groans, rocking against my lips, sliding over my tongue.

"Goddamn, Brooke. Your mouth is unreal."

I want to show him how good he makes me feel. How powerful in a world that tried to take it away.

But he's determined when he shifts me up the

bed on my back. Lifts my knee, pulls it around his hip, and positions himself at my entrance. "Look at me."

I couldn't look away.

As he sinks in, my mouth falls open at the feel of him.

It's a leap of faith. The stretch as he fills me.

"That's it. Wanna touch every inch of you."

My eyes drift closed as he moves forward until he's all the way in.

I get a moment to experience the sensation. Until he pulls back, then he drives back in. The rhythm is too slow to be a race, and he's too deep to be comfortable.

"You're mine."

He mumbles it so low, I'm not sure I've heard it.

But pleasure takes over and I'm clinging to him. My climax comes first. Then he's clenched tight everywhere, his jaw, his shoulders.

Pleasure rips through him, and I love knowing I caused it. But I can't focus on it because we're both falling, tumbling through the atmosphere.

I love being helpless with him.

Minutes later, I'm catching my breath when he reaches over to put out the candle.

"Happy New Year, Princess," he murmurs in my ear.

It's going to be.

His arms wrap around me, tugging my back to his front.

His heart beats through my back. The rhythm matches mine.

23

MILES

"*S*hit, that hurt." Rookie winces as he watches a video version of himself take a hard foul.

"Happened two days ago. You should be good as new." Atlas throws a pencil at him that bounces off his shoulder.

"Says the guy who took his sweet time coming back this year."

Today's our day off in between road games and the Kodiaks are packed into a meeting room watching film after practice.

I'm in the back row with Rookie.

Jay picked the front without so much as a glance my way.

Chloe knocks on the door. "Can I have a word?"

Coach nods. "We're just wrapping up here." One more look sweeps the room. "I mean what I said. Keep it clean. No risks. We're playing second-half basketball now."

He steps back and Chloe smiles, taking the floor.

"Didn't know you were traveling with us this week." Jay shifts forward in his seat.

"The communications team has some decisions to make. The GM thought it would be best if I attended in person but I'm heading back after this."

Chloe lifts her iPad, swiping a finger over the surface to pull up her notes. She's not a big person, especially compared to us, but the suit jacket is a "don't fuck with me" reminder.

Jay and Chloe dated before my time. I'm not privy to the full details of exactly what went down, but from a couple of times he's confided after he's had a few drinks, their breakup nearly destroyed him.

Not that you'd know it from the outside. Jayden's the perfect modern point guard. He's personable and professional, the guy who can flex with a veteran player or take a hard line to show a new one how it's done.

Reporters like joking around with me, but when the media need a real answer after a game about how the team views their play, they go to Jay. They trust him.

So do I.

But in the couple of weeks since he found out about me and Brooke, there's a new ice age that's descended on the team.

I've been trying to give him space to process, figuring he'll thaw out. In the meantime, there are real stakes for the team, and me. My agent hasn't heard back from the shoe sponsor and the Kodiaks are hovering in the last Western playoff spot.

"Voting for the all-star game is coming up. We need to finalize who we're putting forward," Chloe says.

The East and West teams will be made up of guys from across the league. Even though it doesn't contribute toward anything in the regular season, it's a big deal, both for pride and a player's marketability. My own agent has told me that it can add millions a year in negotiation power.

Though the choice of which players will make up the roster is ultimately made by coaches, media and fans, it's customary that the PR engine of each pro team campaigns hard for a couple of their guys. Most teams wind up with one player who makes the cut, but others can get selected for the peripheral contests.

I've been for the three-point competition. It was a lot of fun to participate, though it's more of a spectacle and bragging rights than anything.

"We decided we're going to push for Miles," Chloe says.

Scattered hollers go up around the room. Rookie thumps me on the back.

It takes a moment for the words to sink in. I never pictured myself as a legit all-star, though on paper, I'm turning in the kind of games that put my name in the mix.

My first thought is: *I can't wait to tell Brooke.*

She's at home this week and her friend Ruby is scheduled to visit from New York. She's been looking forward to seeing her friend since they decided on it a few days ago. I'm glad they're going to get some time together. Between working her ass off finding new gigs and helping Nova with her bookings—not to mention talking me down when I get up in my head about for this shoe contract—she deserves a break.

"What about Clay?" Jay interrupts.

The hollers die down.

Our tattooed forward, occupying a seat in Jay's

row, shakes his head. "I've been to the all-star game enough years. Nova and I are going to the beach."

Jay looks around. "Is there anyone else in contention?"

Chloe clears her throat. "I'm not looking for nominations, Jayden."

Two guys in the row ahead exchange looks, probably at her using his full name.

"Besides," she goes on. "Garrett deserves it. Anyone else have comments?"

There's only support from the rest, but by the end of the meeting, one thing's clear.

If I thought Jay was thawing toward me, I was wrong.

BROOKE

I'm waiting at the airport when Ruby gets off the plane in her cashmere sweatsuit and oversized Versace sunglasses.

"I need an eye mask. My dark circles are about to declare their own zip codes," says my friend.

"You look fucking fantastic."

We hug, and love washes over me. It's only been a month since I saw her face, but I missed her like crazy.

"I have a spa visit booked," I say.

"Thought you were short on cash?" she asks as I insist on taking her carry-on bag. We head through the airport to the parking garage.

"I've been working for Nova. And I just got paid for this *Vivaro* campaign." The funds hit my bank account, alleviating the ever-present fear of whether a new partner will actually follow through and pay you what they promised, when they promised it.

We drop off her bag and head to the spa together. I've been looking forward to this since I booked it.

At the front, we fill out the forms. Then I produce a credit card.

The sales associate waves. "Oh, no. It's already been covered."

"By whom?" I ask.

"Mr. Garrett says it's his treat."

Ruby's eyebrows rise through her hairline, but she waits to ask questions.

"So catch me up," Ruby says as we take our spots next to each other for pedicures.

"I've been dating... Giles," I say, changing Miles's name deliberately so we're not overheard and turned into gossip fodder.

"Dating, huh? It's been a minute for you."

I fan through the color swatches. Pink. Purple. "I mean, we're already living together, so that's practically the same thing."

"It's not and you know it. There are levels of intimacy that have nothing to do with where you brush your teeth and where he does."

I grimace. "Different bathrooms. I don't share with guys—"

"You know what I mean. Are you in love with him?"

"That's a little excessive." I decide on a pink and start to hand back the swatches, but I linger on a blue one. The color of his eyes.

"So wait, dating publicly?"

"It came out recently."

"What about... Bey." She goes with my naming convention.

"Bey is not speaking to me and barely to Giles."

Ruby snorts loudly enough that her pedicure tech glances up, startled. "He was always easily offended."

"Thank you! He has to fix the universe the way he likes it," I confirm. "The team is off playing on the road and, judging by a clip I saw online last night, my brother is making it worse on the court."

"I'm sorry. Have you talked to him about it?"

"It seems like a face to face thing. But between the team's practices and travel, he's impossible to get hold of." I shift in my seat. "How's Tim?"

"He wants to go back to school. Says he held down the fort while I was finishing med school, so it's his turn."

"And you don't want him to?" I guess.

Her lips twitch. "I got offered the promotion. The one that would take me off night shifts."

"Rube, that's amazing! Wait, is it more hours?"

"Not on paper. But it is more scrutiny. I'd be heading up a trauma group, be the public face. I need to pay attention to the details. Tim doesn't like taking risks."

"Too bad. We're risk takers, Rubes." I clink my glass against hers, and she grins.

"To the risk takers."

After our pedicures are finished, the techs show us back out to the lounge.

I send a text to Miles, telling him thank you for the spa day. On impulse, I include a photo of my toes with the blue polish. He won't answer until later because he has a game, but I want to let him know I'm thinking of him.

Yet somehow, I get a text back almost immediately.

Miles: You're welcome, Princess.

I'm grinning so wide it hurts.
Maybe Ruby's right. Maybe this is love.

"That's quite the package." Ruby nods toward the massive cardboard box in my room.

We've finished our takeout dinner and Waffles is making a play for Ruby to take him home, huffing happily at her feet as she scratches his ears.

"Clothes from *Vivaro*," I confirm. I just started going through them this week and picking out some pieces for my next posts.

I open up my social media to show her their page.

There's a new message in my DMs. Normally I wait until I have a minute to answer them, but this one's from a familiar name.

I click on her profile and realize it's another creator in a similar space.

Hi Brooke! I hope it's okay that I reached out. I saw that you were promoting *Vivaro* too, and I wondered if you've had any issues with them?

I frown as I type back.

Hey Alicia! They've been great so far, but it's still new. What kind of problems have you encountered?

The sound of the condo front desk calling on my phone interrupts my thoughts.

"You expecting company?" Ruby asks.

"Not that I know of."

I hit accept and listen to the concierge. "Of course! Send her up."

I bounce across the condo to the front door.

When I open it, Chloe's standing on the other side with a bottle of wine. "Thank you for your help at New Year's. This is for you, but it looks like you started already."

Ruby laughs from behind me. I introduce them.

"We're going out tonight," I inform Chloe.

"You should come!" Ruby insists.

Chloe laughs. "I can't."

"Ruby is a doctor. She'll make sure we don't die," I say.

"Oh, no. I assume zero responsibility for either of you."

"That's not why. The team has a game."

Ruby turns on the TV. "Hate to tell you, but it looks like it might be a blowout."

An hour later, we're off to a club.

I text Miles to say sorry about the game but that he played amazing.

"You used to date Brooke's brother, right?" Ruby calls over the music.

"A long time ago," Chloe says.

"How do we get him to chill the fuck out?"

Chloe laughs. "He's chill about a lot of things, but loyalty is a big deal to him. It's why he's such a good team player. He takes the time to understand each guy and has a particular relationship with each of them. But when someone disappoints him, he lets them know it."

"He wants his people to be *his* people," I cut in.

"He was like this growing up. He was the oldest and he wanted to make every decision."

"So maybe Miles lets Jay get a free shot in, then everyone's good?" Ruby flips her palms.

"First, I thought you were a doctor?" Chloe says.

"Doctor, yes. Problem solver...also yes."

"Fair enough. But no violence." Chloe winces. "The league does not look kindly on that sort of thing."

I reach for my drink and take a long sip.

"How worried are you?" I ask Chloe.

"The loss tonight means they slip another spot down the standings. The worst case scenario is they miss the playoffs."

Shit.

I'm still turning that over when my phone vibrates with a video call. *Miles.* The game must be long over. I hit Accept.

"Hi!" I holler over the club noise.

"Been looking at your pic from the spa."

"You have a foot fetish?"

"Didn't know that about myself, but I might now. Where are you?" His image is blurry.

I tell him I went out with Ruby and Chloe, or try to.

"So, I can't tuck you in."

I shift out of the booth and bite my lip, pushing through the club to get to a dark hallway where it's quieter. "Want to see what I got?" I put the phone down my pants.

"Damn. I saw... nothing." He grins sheepishly and my heart threatens to beat out of my chest. "How's your visit with Ruby?"

His thoughtfulness catches me by surprise.

"Epic. Especially thanks to you."

Kevin was always snobby and self-centred. Miles is kind and caring. He had a rough game, but he looks as if there's nowhere he'd rather be than talking to me.

"Oh. Chloe said they're going to campaign me for the all-star game."

I screech. "That's incredible! You deserve it."

"I keep looking around to see if someone's pulling a prank. You know, after all the years I pulled them on other people." He grins.

Pride and warmth wash over me. "You're incredible."

His brow furrows, like he can't see or hear me or both. "What?"

"Nothing! I'll see you in a couple days."

"Night, Princess."

I clutch my phone to my chest like a teenager with a crush.

Only my crush happens to be a pro basketball player who's sexy as hell with a heart of gold who'd move mountains for me.

If this is what it feels like to fall hard? Maybe it's worth the risk.

24

BROOKE

"*I* need advice and I wasn't sure where else to go."

My mom stares back at me from the other side of her office door. She dismisses her aide, and the woman slips out with a nod to me.

"About dating the basketball player?" Mom continues when the woman is out of earshot.

"No," I enunciate crisply. "It's about this collaboration. Another creator reached out to me because she was having problems with the company. Since yesterday, she's put me in touch with a few more creators with the same experience."

Mom waves me in and closes the door behind me. She ignores the desk and chairs and crosses to a couch, perching on one end. "What specifically seems to be the problem?"

I sink onto the seat, crossing my knees instead of my ankles and ignoring her look that follows the movement. "The company has had lags in subsequent payments. They blame it on the banks but it appears to be a consistent pattern, because all of the creators have had at least one successful payment. Then, creators submit photos for consideration but *Vivaro* won't approve them. They go back with endless requests and hurdles. One of the creators, Alicia, later found they used her post after all in a print campaign and didn't even credit her."

"But so far they've followed through on all of their commitments to you."

"So far."

It's possible these are isolated issues and won't affect me. Still, when I went through the company's collaboration posts for the past several months, nearly half of the creators were ones cited by Alicia as having encountered problems even though none of them posted about it publicly.

"Why did these creators come to you?" Mom asks.

"I don't know." It's a question I've asked myself but haven't been able to answer.

"I don't want to see you involved in this. It's always been challenging for people who look like us to gain the same visibility and profile. If you push on this, you absolutely risk losing the partnership. More than that, it could affect your reputation and chances at future work."

She's not wrong, but something about her words rings false.

"Isn't this a perfect example of why we should stand up? It's one thing to build a brand for myself, but I want to see everyone succeed. Creators have less power and resources than big companies. Those companies need to be held to account. Isn't that what you've always campaigned on?"

My mother's eyes soften. "Part of making change is picking the right battles. I don't recommend that you pick this one."

Though some of the women have a smaller following than me, Alicia's is comparable. If they looked me up online, they would have found information about my sorority, my upbringing, my family.

"Maybe they came to me because I'm your

daughter. Because they thought you raised me to help people."

She folds her arms as if she's about to chastise me.

In the end, she sighs. "If you do take this one, you need to be careful about it. Impulsivity won't serve you."

I lift my chin.

On my way out, she clears her throat.

"Before you go, I'd like to ask a favor. It turns out I can't do things alone, either."

25

BROOKE

The brown paper package is tucked carefully under my arm like the latest designer handbag. It was couriered over for Miles from his agent's office, and I offered to bring it by the arena, since he's going to be in team stuff all day.

Security recognizes me and lets me through with a wave. I head toward the practice area, the sounds of squeaking shoes and basketballs guiding me.

When I reach the end of the hall, florescent lights illuminate the Kodiaks in practice jerseys, working through drills at both ends of the court. All the guys are working hard, but my attention slides to Miles.

He's cutting through the defense, shoulder to shoulder with Clay, putting up shots a perimeter player has no business getting. But he's been asked to do more this year, to be two guys really, and he's doing it.

Coach blows his whistle and the guys head for the sidelines.

Except Miles. He looks for me.

When he jogs over, I say, "Hi. I didn't want to interrupt practice but I wanted to bring you this."

He brushes his lips across my cheek before he opens the package, his brows lifting. "What is... Shit."

The blue basketball shoe is sleek and sculpted. The sponsor's logo is on the side, but it's the name across the heel that has him gripping the sole tighter.

Miles's name.

"No way," he says.

His agent called shortly after the Kodiaks released their campaign for Miles to make the all-star game on social media.

Miles and I sat together, him on the couch and me curled in his lap, and went through the details line by line until the early hours of the morning.

"I know you still have to finalize the deal," I say, "but they wanted you to see a prototype."

The sponsor wants to keep it under wraps until

the all-star game in the hopes that he'd be named a player.

He gets a bunch of cash when the deal is announced, and a bonus if he's named an all-star.

"Grams is never going to believe they're putting my name on a basketball shoe. She'll think I made it up." Miles's voice is full of awe.

"Then I'll tell her it's legit."

I throw my arms around Miles, and he lifts me off my feet. When he sets me back down, he kisses me. His mouth is hot and hungry, but he gives as much as he takes. His fingers thread in my hair as though he can't get enough.

"This wouldn't have happened without you." He says it against my mouth.

Part of me wants to argue, but a bigger part wants to absorb all of this moment.

My fingers slip against his bare shoulders, which are still damp from sweat. I give zero fucks.

The sounds of laughter and conversation and sneakers registers too late.

The rest of the Kodiaks sweeps down the hall, en route to the locker room. Jay spots us, his gaze going cool.

Miles stiffens, and I squeeze his hand before calling after my brother.

"Hey. Got a second?"

I slip out of Miles's hands and start toward my brother.

He shakes his head. "Not now."

"Jay. Come on—"

"Not right now." He turns his back on me and silently follows his team to the locker room.

MILES

"This a palace or what?" I ask as we step into the next room.

I'm taking Grams on a tour of a new retirement home. They have around-the-clock care if needed, activities every hour of the day including ballroom dancing, and the best food in the state. I know because I read all the reviews.

With the shoe deal, I'll be able to keep her in the best standard of care as long as she needs it.

But it's a nonstarter if she doesn't want to be here.

"There's a games room. I don't need a whole room for games," she says lightly.

"Personally, I have found games to be very fulfilling. Also lucrative."

Her eyes crinkle at the corners.

"You don't like what they have? I'll get you foosball," I say.

Brooke comes around the corner. "The bathrooms are definitely first class. Oooh, cards. Want to test it out? You seem like a woman who can beat the house at poker."

She helps my grandmother into a seat and takes one next to her. Brooke deals, the two of them deciding on rules with a few quick exchanges, then they play a hand as if I'm not even there.

My heart kicks at the sight of my girl and the woman who's my closest family smiling and teasing and laughing.

With a few days straight in Denver, I've been trying to get Grams's housing arrangements sorted out. Soon it'll be all-star break.

Pressure in the Kodiaks organization is dialing up, on and off court. We're not at the top of our division, but we're clinging to a playoff spot. Our plan for the post-season has to be hammered out in a matter of days, but more personal concerns are hanging over my head.

"You two going to deal me in?"

"Ante up, honey," Grams says.

"We're playing for gum," Brooke informs me.

I pull a hundred dollar bill from my wallet.

Brooke and Grams exchange a look.

"High roller," Brooke says.

"We can take him," Grams says.

Half an hour later, my grandmother has cleaned us out of cash and gum. She insists on returning the cash to me, stuffing it in my pocket as if I'm ten and she's giving me spending money.

"What do you think?" I ask Grams, leading her out to the car.

"I did like the games."

"Yeah? That's it?"

Her eyes crinkle. "You worry, and I can tell you all day not to, but you're not going to change."

I turn that over as we return my grandmother to her current home.

"I think she liked it," Brooke says, nudging me.

"I think so, too." I pull her under my arm as we walk out. "Enough about my problems. We should get out of here and celebrate your latest campaign. My girl will be the front woman for athleisure in no time."

Once we're back at the car, I glance over to see Brooke staring out the window.

"You okay?" I ask.

She shifts toward me, leaning an elbow against the door. "Vivaro has been behaving unprofessionally with a bunch of creators."

The concern in her voice makes it clear how serious this is to her.

"Tell me."

She does, starting with the complaints from a woman named Alicia. She's put together a document with all of the details.

"I've been hesitating over sending this complaint off, because I'm not sure it's my fight. I'm not sure if I can win. I'm not even sure if it matters."

I cover her hand with mine. "Only thing I'm sure of is that they're lucky to have you speaking for them. You're a badass, Brooke Ellis."

Her lips curve. I can't resist brushing my mouth over them.

"My mom actually gave me good advice for once. Not that it was free." She grimaces. "She wants me to meet Kevin as a favor to her and the campaign."

My hackles rise. He was always an asshole, but as a guy who makes his living with strokes of pens and pieces of paper, it's easy to underestimate how dangerous he is.

"I don't like it."

"You're telling me not to?"

I hiss out a breath. "I'm telling you I'll be watching from the street with my face plastered against the window in case he so much as looks at you wrong."

She laughs. "That's sweet. I'm not going to do it." Her thumb strokes my face. "There's nothing that ties you to him, right? That could come back to hurt you?"

"Nothing." I try not to think of the photographs long buried, focusing instead on the relief on Brooke's face.

"You coming to the game tomorrow?" I ask.

"Boston. It's a big one."

I nod. "Sponsors are going to be there, so I want to put on a show."

"Wouldn't miss it."

26

MILES

"How much does this game matter on a scale of one to ten?"

"Twelve."

Coach's response to the reporter at the pre-game has a finality that resonates through your bones.

Some of the guys keep their heads down before tipoff, but I caught the press conference on my way into the locker room.

We're playing Boston, and Jay's rival, Hawkins. Who finishes first determines who'll get the advantage if we face them in the post-season.

Earlier, it was a question of whether we'd face them due to the luck of the draw. Now, though, it's starting to look like there's a question mark about us even making the playoffs.

It hasn't escaped me that the shoe sponsor is in the stands. I get that they were looking at both me and Hawkins for the deal that'll make sure Grams is taken care of forever, and I want to show them they made the right call.

The tension in the locker room feels as if it's dialed up to a new level.

"Bring it in." Jay motions to us, and we group around him. "It's been a tough road, but we need everyone tonight. Let's get a win. Kodiaks on three."

We shout together, then straighten and file toward the doorway.

The past couple weeks, Jay's been forgoing touching the photo of Waffles, our unofficial locker room mascot. Tonight, he hesitates but touches it on the way out the door.

Hope kicks in my chest.

Maybe this is a turning point.

When we get out there, the crowd is deafening already. I don't see Brooke, Nova, or the others though. The team box has only a few familiar faces, and no Brooke.

From the opening seconds, it's competitive. Boston goes at us hard.

I cut around the court, and Jay finds Atlas in the post early for a layup. *Good start.*

I feed on the sounds of the crowd, the appreciation, then I shut it out and get back to work.

Over the first quarter, Clay gets a dunk.

Rookie gets a pair of threes.

I get another four points in the paint, two of them assisted by Jay.

Clay nods at me as we run back on defense. *Keep going*, he's saying.

There's no better feeling than being what your team needs on any given night, especially a high-stakes one like this. But they need more.

At the end of the first quarter, we've managed to stay up by two.

"... keep working in the paint. Miles, keep grinding against their defense. Wear them down."

We go back out to play the next quarter.

Jay gets called for a foul on Hawkins, and we line up for Boston to shoot two.

The first goes in. *Swish.*

As he puts up the second shot, I look past the net, my eyes landing on the box. Brooke's there with Chloe and Nova and Mari. Brooke waves, and my breathing comes a little easier as my lips twitch. I feel better knowing she's here.

Swish.

"That's fucking *bullshit*."

My attention cuts to Jay standing opposite, staring at me as the ref's whistle shrills.

"Technical foul, Jayden Ellis."

The crowd starts to buzz, confused over Jay's outburst.

"We're playing the most important fucking game of the year and that's what you're thinking about?" he goes on.

There are nine guys ready to play.

Thousands of fans.

Plus a team of refs with all the power.

"Come on, we're going to get a delay of game," I say flatly. I nod to the ref, who's keeping a close eye.

Jay stabs a finger in my chest. "You want everyone to get along, but you don't get to be a selfish prick and still have that happen. You were supposed to be protecting her."

The whistle sounds, the ref teeing us up for delay of game. Groans fill the stadium.

My teeth grind together. "I've been protecting her since the second you asked me to."

"You have no fucking family of your own so you're taking mine."

Jay comes at me, knocking me over. The team descends, pulling us apart.

I try to protect myself. My fist rises to stop Jay

from hitting me, but he moves, and my fist lands in his jaw with a sickening crack.

The ref blows his whistle again, then keeps blowing, a shrill call competing with the crowd.

"You're out of the game, both of you!"

Every man on the Kodiaks bench rises, throwing up their hands. Coach covers his face with his clipboard. The assistants look shocked, their expressions grim.

Fuck.

It's going to be a long night.

27

BROOKE

*W*e always had ice packs in our house growing up. I got comfortable fetching them for my brother for a variety of aches and pains from basketball. Now, I grab one from the coaching staff and wrap it in a towel as I cross to the stadium seat where Miles is perched.

"That was exciting," I say as I slide into the seat next to him.

He leans an elbow on the back of my chair, cocking his head so the stadium lights outline his face, his dimples. "Figured we'd put on a show for you."

It's an hour after the game, and the place has cleared out.

The Kodiaks took a loss. It was foreseeable after

the first quarter. With two starters ejected, it was practically inevitable.

We're all still reeling from it.

"You shouldn't have been ejected from the game." I lift the wrapped pack to the side of his face, and he covers my hand with his.

"They don't like you fighting. Doesn't matter which team it's with." His lips tilt up at one side.

No matter how good an act he's putting on, there will be consequences.

Denver drops a spot in the standings. At this rate, they could miss the playoffs.

As importantly, the fight took place in front of Miles's new sponsor.

Though the deal might be inked, it hasn't been announced yet. Anything could happen.

None of this would have happened if it wasn't for me.

I don't say the words out loud, but it's as if Miles hears them.

He takes my wrist and gently lowers my hand holding the ice pack. "You know this was bound to come to a head."

Was it? I want to shake my brother. He could have fixed this sooner.

"I tried calling him again last night," I admit. "He didn't respond."

Miles nods. "This isn't up to you, Princess. I'm going to fix this thing for good. That's a promise."

Chloe appears on the court, holding her iPad. "Miles. Harlan wants to see you."

GM. Perfect.

Guess he's done with my brother, who he saw first.

"I can wait so we can go home together," I say. "Text me when you're done?"

He brushes his lips over mine before following Chloe toward the hallway.

My feet carry me through the back halls of the building. I bang out half a dozen angry texts to Jay, deleting each.

I hit his contact, bringing up the picture of him. In it, he's wearing a shit-eating grin and a bright pink tie. It was draft night. I picked out his suit, and the moment he was announced during the first round, it was me he looked at. Me he hugged first.

When we were kids, he was always there when I needed him. He brought me into his team. Made me one of them, even when he didn't have to.

One of the guys asked, "Can't you leave your kid sister at home?"

He said, "She's family. Shut your mouth."

Jay has always looked out for me, no matter the cost to him. I want to corner him and demand to know what the hell he's thinking. But then the backs of my eyes burn and I know I'd do something stupid, like ask him if he doesn't love me anymore.

I know he does. He wouldn't be this hurt if he didn't.

I pass the gym, where I collide with a huge form coming out. "Oof."

Clay, I realize when I look up into his square jaw and dark eyes.

"You're here late," I say.

"Just finishing a workout."

The guys work out after playing a full game. Intense conditioning is a part of the job people don't usually appreciate.

He surveys me from my toes to the tip of my head. He's wearing a black tank, his tattoos appearing to spring out of the fabric around his arms and shoulders.

Clay nods to my hand. "I'll show you where that goes."

I'm still holding an ice pack and towel.

He walks down the hall and I fall into step with him, taking two strides for every one of his. Miles is nearly as tall as Clay's six-five, but Clay walks as if he's eight feet tall. He's like a statue of some god, right from his closed-lipped nature to his chiseled body to the art all over him. It could be graffiti.

"Tell me the truth," I hear myself say. "Am I causing problems?"

"You and Garrett aren't making it easier."

The squeak of his sneakers echoes in the hall along with the click of my heels.

"I don't see how it's any of the team's business," I admit.

Clay exhales heavily. "I get it. It's not fair. And I'm not going to stand here and tell you to do one thing when your heart is telling you something opposite."

"I sense a 'but' coming."

"But...there's a window to get things right." Clay shrugs a tattooed shoulder. "People think basketball is forever, but it happens fast. Careers start fast, end fast. Bottom line: the next couple of months matter a lot for the team. If you guys are long-term, ask yourself if it can wait until after the season."

The Kodiaks' all-star and MVP doesn't speak his mind often. I take a moment to process, weighing the words.

"That's probably good advice," I say.

Nova's husband shoots me a wry look. "I sense a 'but' coming."

"But...you're a hypocrite."

Clay straightens, surprise filling his dark eyes. "Me."

"Yes. You fell for Nova. *Hard,* Mr. All-Star-MVP. I watched you do it. Nothing on or off the court was going to get in your way. If you want to preach what you practice, you should be saying 'fuck basketball. Follow your heart.'"

He's quiet a minute. The guy isn't used to people challenging him. "Pretty sure I can't say 'fuck basketball.' That's got to be in my contract somewhere." His lips twitch at the corner. "But maybe you're right about the rest of it."

He takes the ice pack and towel from me and vanishes into the locker room.

28

MILES

"Jay, it's me. Voicemail's a shitty way to do this, but we have to start somewhere and you probably have guard dogs trained on my scent outside your house. I get that you're upset, but we need to talk. This thing is bigger than us and we owe it to the people we care about to figure it out."

~

Kidnapping is never the answer.

Except when it's the only answer.

"We're heading into the most important part of the season and you're acting like idiots. Normally we'd send you to Kodiak Camp to be useful, but you're terrible role models for those kids," Coach snapped the day after the game, when he called me into a meeting. "You can't play, and we can't have you in public."

"What are we supposed to do?"

"Sort your shit out."

Jay and I both scored two-game suspensions and five-figure fines.

The past week, neither of us have been playing games or practicing with the team. It takes three days of lying on my back, staring up at the ceiling while knowing the team is practicing without me before I have the idea.

I don't want to involve Brooke because she'd think it's a nightmare.

"No fucking way," Atlas states when I call him with my request. "I'm injured, but I'll never get back to the team if I help with this because I'll be dead."

"You don't help, you won't have a team to come back to," I warn.

In the end, Clay's the one who comes through and tells the other guys to get onboard.

Atlas throws a bag over his head and puts him in a van, telling him it's a prank. We used to do our share of them, especially back before we took ourselves so seriously.

"Where are we going?" Jay calls from the back seat.

I'm in the front with Atlas, but I don't answer. Don't want him knowing until the last minute.

Atlas drops us off in an area full of snow, surrounded by trees. "Have a good time, man." He tosses me a skeptical look before driving away.

"Who's there?"

I pull the bag off Jay's head.

His confusion and irritation instantly turn to disbelief and anger. "Where the hell are we?"

"Middle of nowhere."

His head swivels wildly as he looks around. "We can't be here."

Laughing probably isn't the best move, but I can't help it. "Actually, we can't be anywhere else. No one wants us."

I give him a moment for that to sink in.

"Atlas helped with this? He's a dead man."

"And Clay. And Rookie." I sigh. "We need peace for the sake of the team. You told me back in college that the team is a family. It's not worth throwing that away over whatever the hell this is."

"Don't lecture me on family. You're the one who stuck yourself in the middle of mine." He paces toward the treelike, kicking at snow as if he wishes it would hurt him back.

"Think what you want about me, but this isn't Brooke's fault. I don't want her hurt."

"You don't get to say that." Jay spins to face me, stabbing a gloved hand in the air. "Mom cut her off, and she told me nothing? But she went to you. Why?"

The change of directions throws me for a beat.

"I honestly don't know. If I had to guess...maybe because she didn't want to disappoint you. Or she didn't want you fixing her problems and she knew you would. You'll always be her big brother."

A sudden gust of wind shakes the trees, sending snow sliding off the needles.

I'm a guy who plays around and doesn't talk a lot about feelings. So instead of trying to make it less of a big deal, I change gears.

"Remember back in college when we did tree planting?" I say. "They explained to us how the root system works. I liked the idea of a tree growing, getting stronger. That trees talk to each other, their roots taking more or less depending on how the trees are growing. I've always done that. I try to make sure everyone's getting along. And I know you do too.

"I didn't realize how fucking thirsty I'd gotten.

Until she was there." I force myself to take a long breath, shoving a hand through my hair until I feel it stick up. "She's been there for years, but the moment she asked me if I'd help with that sorority weekend, the answer was yes. At first I told myself it was because she needed me. Hell, maybe that was part of it, but not all of it. I needed her."

He blinks but doesn't turn away.

"I've wanted her for longer than I should've. If you want to be pissed, be pissed about that. Because the way I feel about her now...there's no helping it. And I wanted to talk to you about it," I go on, not even stopping for breath. "The fact that I couldn't sucked. Because I've never felt like this about anyone. She makes me better, man. I can only hope to do the same for her."

Jay's jaw works, but he doesn't respond.

I run a hand over the tree trunk closest to me, marveling at how it stands up to the winter. Stands up to everything.

"I want to put what's between us aside for the team. If you don't want to trust me again off the court... So be it. But everyone's doubting us, calling us a one-hit wonder. We have to prove that we've still got it."

Jay paces in front of me. There's a good chance

he'll tell me to fuck off. When he stalks toward me, getting right in my face, I think he's going to do more than talk.

"Aright," he says at last.

"We're good?" I can barely hope for it.

"We're teammates. We need to get this back on track or else we'll be watching the playoffs from our sofas."

"And friends?"

He shakes his head. "That's for another day."

It's not everything, but I'll take what I can.

Jay looks around. "It's fucking cold here. How do we get back?"

"We're only twenty minutes from Kodiak Camp."

He curses at me. "Which way?"

I pull out my phone. Then realize there's no signal. "Guess it's good we've got nowhere to be today."

29

BROOKE

The email from Vivaro was brief, pointed, and reeked of lawyers.

We take all allegations very seriously.

We will investigate these claims.

Your contract will be suspended while we do so.

The punchline was clear: no more work with them for the time being, and so no more money coming in. It's probably true that my shot of future collaborations is over, but I decided it's worth the price.

I don't want to be the kind of person who builds a brand while turning a blind eye to the experience of others.

I want to be a woman who'll stand up for other people. It's what I wanted in college, while I was a

Kappa. It's what came out at the retreat, and though I haven't always seen a pathway to being that, this opportunity was clear.

Still, I wish it left me with a warm, fuzzy feeling inside instead of this pit.

It could be that the pit is over what I'm about to do rather than what I've just done.

The Uber pulls up outside the restaurant, a white wood façade with clean, simple and probably expensive lettering. I thank the driver before slipping out.

"Talk to Kevin," Mom said.

"I'd appreciate it," she said.

Despite what Miles and I discussed, I ultimately decided to meet the guy I once thought I loved.

I'm doing it for my mom, but also, the deeper I get with Miles the more I realize I need to clear out what's left of the past.

When I get to our table, it's in a private room.

My flags are going up, but it's only Kevin. I can handle him.

"Thank you," he says with a wide smile when the waitress sets a napkin in his lap. "Still prefer red wine?" he asks me.

"We're here to talk and I don't think it's about

wine. But yes, red is fine," I nod to the waitress, who's already looking between us warily.

Kevin leans back in his seat, sizing me up. "Caroline and I called it off." He pauses to let that sink in. When I don't speak, he continues. "Planning a wedding is so much work, but it turns out canceling one is easy. A couple of calls. Vendors move on. A cascade of bills. Some silence. Then it's over."

"Tragic. We're not meeting to talk about your love life, either."

"Aren't we?"

Caroline dodged a bullet, I want to say. But I swallow it. I get that I'm impulsive, and being polite to him will help people I love.

"She was everything I thought I wanted," he goes on. "Beautiful, of course. Composed. Deliberate."

"Cunning?" I can't resist saying. "You thought you wanted that for a while."

The waitress brings red wine, and I don't stop her when she pours some into my glass. He orders a steak and I get the fish.

"It's strange how you view something differently when it's yours," he says.

"She's not a thing. She's a person." Even I'm not going to let him throw her under the bus.

Kevin takes a sip, frowning into his wine as if it

has disappointed him too. "I always tried to be what my parents wanted. To go into law. I should be partner in a year."

"Congratulations," I say flatly. It would be impossible not to be a partner at your own family's firm. A failure of nepotism.

"I gave up so much, Bee. You know what it's like. I only realized it recently, how you had to give up twice as much to get the same amount back. And I know what you're thinking. We wouldn't have fit."

"Because you cheated on me and left drugs in my room." I lift one of a dozen reasons out of my mind.

His shoulder lifts under the tailored jacket. "We all made mistakes as kids."

I reach for my wine and take a long sip. The warmth distracts me from the conversation.

He talks more bullshit, and I nod sporadically to keep from falling asleep. My mom owes me big time.

"How are you?" he asks as our plates are set in front of us.

"Never better."

"You and that basketball player, huh?"

The hairs on my neck lift. "He's twice the man you are," I say before I can stop it. "He's finally getting the recognition he deserves. Highlight reels. Endorsements. All-star game buzz."

"He made mistakes back then too, Bee." When Kevin's eyes flash, they're gray, like ice.

It occurs to me that Miles's are bright blue, like fire.

"You and I are good at repressing our anger. It comes out in more subtle ways," Kevin says.

My next bite tastes like chalk, but I force it down. "Like sleeping around and snorting piles of cocaine?"

He laughs. "Touché."

He's so goddamned smug. But as he cuts his steak, there's a recklessness to him.

"Those things are easily buried. Miles, on the other hand, snapped in a way you can't come back from."

I realize I'm just pushing my rice pilaf into piles at this point. "It was a long time ago."

"I agree. And I think we should bury the hatchet, as it were."

"Or what?" I set down my fork.

"Or some of that long-buried history might come up." He grins, all white teeth. Like a shark.

It's a threat.

I might not know exactly what he's threatening but I sense it.

My past has hung with me a long time. I never imagined Miles had anything to hide.

The image of Kevin with his face pummeled flashes across my mind—the work of Miles's fists when he was a rookie and I was a college junior.

If Miles does have secrets, it's because of me.

I wait until our waitress is out of earshot to rise. "This dinner is over. I'll let you get the bill."

30

BROOKE

"*L*ast week was fun." Chloe's voice has me looking up from the empty conference room I ducked into to check my email.

"The part where a fight broke out on court over me and two starting players got suspended?"

The Kodiaks have a game in a few hours, but I came early to try and catch my brother. When Jay's stressed, he always likes to hit the gym before a game to stretch.

"No, the part where you, me and Ruby went out." She laughs. "I heard Miles and Jay struck an agreement."

"Supposedly. Miles said it was top secret guy stuff. I guess we'll see what happens on the court."

"Well, it seems like everything you're around

turns to gold. Nova's thrilled with her new opportunities. And a few of the connections you helped to make at the New Year's party have already led to new partnership conversations for the team."

"That's fantastic," I say, genuinely pleased.

She tilts her head. "You know, I'm trying to hire someone in PR to help me. It's been hard finding the right person, but since New Year's, I can't help thinking maybe the perfect person has been under my nose the whole time."

"Me." I say it out loud because I'm honestly not sure.

Chloe laughs. "Yes, you."

"You want me around here *more often*? Did you see the drama over the past month?"

"I did. And as much as they don't always act it, they're professionals. They'll figure out their business."

My heart beats harder. This could be a stellar opportunity. I respect Chloe, and I could learn a lot from her. Plus, I know basketball, and the Kodiaks' budget blows Elise's company or Vivaro out of the water.

"I need to think about it."

Chloe's face splits into a smile. "Of course. If it

helps, I'll email over an offer to let you know what I was thinking. But don't take too long."

I go back out into the hall and run straight into my brother. "Hi."

"Hey."

"Your suspension over?"

"First game back is tonight. But you knew that." He lifts a brow.

I fold my arms, the offer still under one. If this is going to work, I need to make this right. "Listen, about what went down—"

"I know you're going to give me shit for stepping in where I don't belong."

"I was going to say that if Miles and me together seemed like sneaking around or changed the team dynamic, I'm sorry. You've built up a lot of trust together, and you need that for things to work on the court."

"Yeah, well." Jay's eyes widen a little as he adjusts his bag on his shoulder. "Guess he always had a thing for you."

"Can you blame him? I'm amazing."

Jay snorts, but I get the half smile I'm after.

I bite my lip as I recall what Kevin said to me. His barely veiled threat over dinner.

"The suspension you both got... how much

trouble is that really?"

Jay frowns. "Neither of us are going anywhere, if that's what you're worried about. I've got some goodwill saved up here, and so does he. We pay our fines and eat whatever shit Coach doles out, and we'll be back in business."

"So you're not losing your job, but it was strike one," I read.

"Sure. But this isn't baseball. We don't get three."

We need to be on our best behavior. Jay doesn't need to spell it out for me.

If the Kodiaks as defending champs don't even make the playoffs, it would be dire for the entire organization. It would affect not only Miles but my brother, Clay by extension Nova, Chloe.

I think back to Clay's comments that there's a narrow window for Jay and Miles to do this right. I want the team to prove themselves this year, to have a chance to go back for the championship, not least because Miles's role is that much bigger this year. He's not only part of the story, he's writing it.

"Least it was on the court," my brother goes on. "It looks bad, but you can blame it on adrenaline. Off the court is something else."

I turn that over. "Have you seen him today?"

"He should be here soon. We're getting ready for shoot around." My brother sends off a text.

"He's not answering. At least he's not answering me." I hold up my phone with the message I sent Miles a couple hours ago.

Jay blocks the screen with a hand. "I don't want to see it."

"Relax. This is a dick-pic-free zone."

He makes a pained sound.

"You guys text each other back right away, huh?" he grumbles.

"Yeah."

"Cute." But he shakes his head.

"Hey." I kick a toe against his shoe. "Are we good?"

"Are you happy?"

"Mhmm."

He cocks his head. "I just don't want this to go bad. For you, for the team, for anyone."

"You worry too much."

Chloe comes barreling down the hall, iPad clutched in one hand and phone in the other. "Get outside. Now."

Jay and I exchange a startled look.

"What's happening?" I demand.

She doesn't answer and is halfway to the end of the hall. We follow, our footsteps echoing.

"Chlo," Jay calls.

He catches up to her first, me a moment later. I've never seen her move this fast. Never seen anyone move this fast outside a race or a basketball game, if I'm honest.

We burst out the front doors, Chloe leading the way. She pulls up fast enough I run into her back.

The pavilion in front of the stadium holds a scene that takes me a full minute to process.

First I see Miles.

My heart lifts, as it always does when I see him. He's got his bag over one shoulder, a puffer coat unzipped and his hair wavy around his face.

But something's wrong.

His hands are balled into fists and he's talking with someone. *Shouting* at someone.

The other man is in a wool coat, his cheeks pink and pale hair wispy. His face is pulled into an aristocratic sneer.

Not just anyone.

Kevin.

"What is he doing here?" Jay says what we're all thinking.

Nothing good.

The way they're arguing is dangerous.

I can't overhear the words, but a crowd is gathering.

"Miles!" I call.

He turns toward me, his expression torn. Then whatever Kevin says has him turning back.

Phones are lifted, taking photos and video, as if they know they're going to see what they came for.

Or rather what they didn't.

Miles throws the first punch.

Everything slows down.

Not enough time for me to run to them and tell people to put down their phones, to stop filming.

Kevin responds with an upper cut.

Miles hits back.

I'm frozen. I can't believe what I'm seeing.

My brother hollers something I can't hear.

Clay is there too.

Sirens wail in the distance, coming closer.

It's over.

It's over for Miles, and it's all my fault.

Thank you for reading ***Hard to Take***. I hope

you're enjoying Miles and Brooke's sexy, emotional romance!

Their story concludes in **Hard to Break** (coming Fall 2024).

My teammate's little sister is all I've ever wanted.
Now, I'll do whatever it takes to keep her.

For writing updates, early excerpts and exclusive giveaways...
Join my VIP List and never miss a thing!
www.piperlawsonbooks.com/subscribe

BOOKS BY PIPER LAWSON

FOR A FULL LIST PLEASE GO TO
PIPERLAWSONBOOKS.COM/BOOKS

KING OF THE COURT SERIES

After being dumped and losing my job the same week, the last thing my broken heart needs is a rebound.

A steamy, grumpy sunshine sports romance featuring a woman down on her luck, a star basketball player with a filthy mouth, and a connection neither of them can deny.

OFF-LIMITS SERIES

Turns out the beautiful man from the club is my new professor... But he wasn't when he kissed me.

Off-Limits is a forbidden age gap college romance series. Find out what happens when the beautiful man from the club is Olivia's hot new professor.

WICKED SERIES

Rockstars don't chase college students. But Jax Jamieson never followed the rules.

Wicked is a new adult rock star series full of nerdy girls, hot rock stars, pet skunks, and ensemble casts you'll want to be friends with forever.

RIVALS SERIES

At seventeen, I offered Tyler Adams my home, my life, my heart. He stole them all.

Rivals is an angsty new adult series. Fans of forbidden romance, enemies to lovers, friends to lovers, and rock star romance will love these books.

ENEMIES SERIES

I sold my soul to a man I hate. Now, he owns me.

Enemies is an enthralling, explosive romance about an American DJ and a British billionaire. If you like wealthy, royal alpha males, enemies to lovers, travel or sexy romance, this series is for you!

TRAVESTY SERIES

My best friend's brother grew up. Hot.

Travesty is a steamy romance series following best friends who start a fashion label from NYC to LA. It contains best friends brother, second chances, enemies to lovers, opposites attract and friends to lovers stories. If you like sexy, sassy romances, you'll love this series.

PLAY SERIES

I know what I want. It's not Max Donovan. To hell with his money, his gaming empire, and his joystick.

Play is an addictive series of standalone romances with slow burn tension, delicious banter, office romance and unforgettable characters. If you like smart, quirky, steamy enemies-to-lovers, contemporary romance, you'll love Play.

MODERN ROMANCE SERIES

When your rich, handsome best friend asks you to be his fake girlfriend? Say no.

Modern Romance is a smart, sexy series of contemporary romances following a set of female friends running a relationship marketing company in NYC. If you enjoy hot guys who treat their families like gold, fun antics, dirty talk, real characters, steamy scenes, badass heroines and smart banter, you'll love the Modern Romance series.

Devon Burke: I think I'm in the Million Commas Spliced Club now. I don't know why you still say yes when I ask you to read for me, but I send up thanks every time.

Annette Brignac: Thank you for caring about me when I forget. I probably have not had any water to drink yet today, but I know I will, because you'll remind me. I do not deserve you.

Kate Tilton: Thank you for rolling with it. This industry can seem as if it changes daily, and I'm ever grateful for you bringing your positive, capable self to...whatever it is we do here.

Lori Jackson and Emily Wittig: You make beautiful pictures from my rants. Thank you for responding to my emails when I ask for one more tweak three months after you've forgotten who I am.

Georgana Grinstead, Kim, Christina, Sarah, and the entire VPR team: You make the complicated work of publishing seem effortless. Thank you for your wisdom, genius, and tireless effort to help readers find books they'll love.

ACKNOWLEDGMENTS

Thank you for reading Hard to Take! I hope you're loving Miles and Brooke's steamy, fun, and a little twisty best friend's brother story.

This book wouldn't have happened without the support of my awesome readers, including my ARC readers. Thank you for providing endless enthusiasm, cheerleading, early feedback, and help spreading the word.

Becca Mysoor: Thank you for being a friend to my characters, but mostly, for being *my* friend.

Cassie Robertson: You always seem to laugh with me rather than at me. Which, considering some of the things I send you in drafts, is truly remarkable.

Dria Roland: Thank you for being such a brilliant storyteller and a gracious human. And for sharing both of those with me.

amazon.com/author/piperlawson

bookbub.com/authors/piper-lawson

instagram.com/piperlawsonbooks

facebook.com/piperlawsonbooks

goodreads.com/piperlawson

ABOUT THE AUTHOR

Piper Lawson is a WSJ and USA Today bestselling author of smart and steamy romance.

She writes women who follow their dreams, best friends who know your dirty secrets and love you anyway, and complex heroes you'll fall hard for.

Piper lives in Canada with her tall and brilliant husband. She's a sucker for dark eyes, dark coffee, and dark chocolate.

For a complete reading list, visit
www.piperlawsonbooks.com/books

Subscribe to Piper's VIP email list
www.piperlawsonbooks.com/subscribe